DEAD TO RIGHTS

AN ASHLAND NOVEL

JESSICA PRINCE

To the ladies who like their guys to be rough around the edges and have a real gift for dirty talk.
Pope is for you.

LET'S CONNECT

Let's Connect

By signing up for my newsletter, you're guaranteeing you'll stay up to date on all new releases, cover reveals, giveaways, sales, and all the other exciting book news I have coming!

I pinky-promise to use my emails for good only, not to spam you, and make sure each one is enjoyable for everybody.

Sign up on my website at www.authorjessicaprince.com

A NOTE FROM THE AUTHOR

After starting my Redemption series, I began getting messages asking if a particular character or "club" was going to get a book. Well, I'm so stinking excited to finally be giving you Pope's story, book one in my brand-new Ashland series!

Now, there's something I feel I need to say about this series before you dive in. Yes, this is Pope's story, the president of the Iron Wraith's motorcycle club. And yes, this series will also be featuring other club members. But with that being said, this is NOT a motorcycle club series.

It isn't that I dislike MC series—I'm actually a massive fan and have read and re-read several. But as many of you know, I tend to fall hard for my secondary characters, and I didn't want to risk limiting myself or forcing myself into a corner where I have to create yet another spin-off series when I still have so much to come in the future.

While I love these Wraiths, and know you will too, once you dive into this story, you'll understand why I didn't want to limit myself to just the club when there are other heroes you'd want to hear from.

With that said, go forth and enjoy! I can't wait for you to get to really know Pope, and I promise this story was totally worth the wait!

• Jess

DISCOVER OTHER BOOKS BY JESSICA

ASHLAND SERIES
Dead to Rights

WHITECAP SERIES
Crossing the Line
My Perfect Enemy
Turn of the Tides

WHISKEY DOLLS SERIES
Bombshell
Knockout
Stunner
Seductress
Temptress
Vamp

Rising from the Ashes
Pushing the Boundaries
Worth the Wait

THE COLORS NOVELS:
Scattered Colors
Shrinking Violet
Love Hate Relationship
Wildflower

THE LOCKLAINE BOYS (a LOVE HATE RELATIONSHIP spinoff):
Fire & Ice
Opposites Attract
Almost Perfect

THE PEMBROOKE SERIES (a WILDFLOWER spinoff):
Sweet Sunshine
Coming Full Circle
A Broken Soul

CIVIL CORRUPTION SERIES
Corrupt
Defile
Consume
Ravage

<u>**GIRL TALK SERIES:**</u>

Seducing Lola

Tempting Sophia

Enticing Daphne

Charming Fiona

<u>**STANDALONE TITLES:**</u>

One Knight Stand

Chance Encounters

Nightmares from Within

<u>**DEADLY LOVE SERIES:**</u>

Destructive

Addictive

DEAD TO RIGHTS PLAYLIST

"I Deserve a Drink" by Morgan Wallen

"Last Night" by Morgan Wallen"

"Edge of Seventeen" by Stevie Nicks

"The Fire" by Chris Stapleton

"White Horse" by Christ Stapleton

"Burning Man" by Dierks Bentley and Brothers Osborne

"I'm Comin' Over" by Chris Young

"One Number Away" by Luke Combs

"Higher" by Chris Stapleton

"Hurricane" by Luke Combs

"Crosswind" by Chris Stapleton

"Something in the Orange" by Zach Bryan

"Games" by Luke Bryan

"Girl Like You" by Jason Aldean

"We're An American Band" by Grand Funk Railroad

"Paint It, Black" by the Rolling Stones

"House of the Rising Sun" by The Animals
"Ramble On" by Led Zeppelin
"The Chain" by Fleetwood Mac
"Have You Ever Seen the Rain" by Creedence Clearwater Revival
"Wild Horses" by The Rolling Stones

ONE

HUH. *Well, this tracks*, I thought to myself as I stood on the side of the road with my hands on my hips, staring down at my blown tire. It figured something like this would happen, like karma had just been waiting to kick me while I was down. A giant FU from the universe for something I must have done in a past life.

My fingers curled, creating white-knuckled fists as I struggled to stuff down the frustrated scream trying to claw its way up my throat. I wanted to throw my middle fingers in the air and rage at whatever higher power was currently using me as their own personal punching bag, not that it would have done me any good. I still would have been right where I was, flat tire and all.

It wasn't that I didn't know how to change a tire; my father insisted I had to learn before I ever got my license. The problem was that all of my belongings, everything I had to my name, was crammed into my car, taking up every bit of free space I had, so getting to the spare was going to be a nightmare.

Heaving a sigh, I pressed the button on my key fob to open the liftgate as I pulled the phone from my back pocket and scrolled to the name I'd stored in my contacts weeks ago.

The call connected on the second ring. "Hi, Iris. It's Lennon."

My realtor's smiling voice came through the line as I tucked the phone between my ear and shoulder and started pulling my stuff out of the back hatch, lining it carefully along the side of the road so I could get to the spare in the back.

"Hey! How are you? You almost here?"

I pushed a breath out through my nose and closed my eyes, struggling to find my calm and keep a tight grasp on it.

"Well . . . almost. I'm just calling to tell you I'm going to be a little late meeting you at the house. I'm really sorry." My sentence ended on a grunt as the particularly heavy suitcase I'd just tugged on tumbled from the back of my car. "Son of a bitch," I hissed, nearly dropping my phone as I jumped back to avoid my toes being squished.

"Are you okay?"

"Yeah, sorry." I pursed my lips and blew at a strand of hair that had fallen into my eyes. "I made it to town, but I got a flat tire. Now I'm stuck on the side of the road in . . ." I lifted my head and turned in a slow circle, taking in my surroundings as I raked a hand through my hair, "the middle of freaking nowhere."

It was definitely going to take a bit of time for me to acclimate to my new environment. I'd been a city girl my whole life, so used to big-box stores, a Starbucks on every corner, fast-food chains, and malls. But that wasn't my life anymore.

I'd taken the first job offer to teach middle school English that came my way after my divorce had finalized, the farther from the world I was leaving behind, the better. That was how I'd ended up here in Ashland, a small town hundreds of miles from everything I'd once known, and where motorcycles apparently outnumber regular cars three to one.

"Oh no. Do you need help? I have the number if you need a tow—"

"No, that's all right." I let out another grunt as I got the suitcase right side up, moved it aside, and went back for more. "I've got it. I'll probably have the tire changed before the tow truck could even get here anyway. I just have to unload the back of my car to get to the tire so it'll take longer than it normally would. I totally understand if you have things to do and can't wait at the house. I can meet you at your office to get the keys if you prefer."

"Please. Don't worry about it. Just take your time and be careful. I'll be waiting when you finally get here."

I let out a breath, my shoulders drooping in relief. "Thank you so much. You're the best."

"Don't mention it. Just be safe. I'll see you in a bit."

I hung up the phone and stuffed it back into my pocket so I could get down to business. By the time I had everything emptied and could reach the spare, beads of sweat were gathered along my hairline and trickling down my spine, amplifying my discomfort and annoyance. My shirt was sticking to my sweaty back and my hair was falling into my eyes and getting stuck on my forehead as I struggled to loosen the spare.

This whole disaster was so on-brand for how shit in my life had been going in recent months. When I looked back on the dreams I'd had for my life, I pictured a happy marriage, a job I loved, and maybe a couple kids one day after my husband and I had finished traveling and decided it was time to settle down. But those dreams had gone up in a puff of smoke when I left work early one day with a nasty head cold, only to come home and find my husband with his dick shoved down the throat of one of my closest friends, a woman who had been one of my bridesmaids when we'd gotten married.

That was a sight no woman could ever unsee, and after everything I'd gone through in the aftermath of that betrayal, I was finally ready to start my new life. Of course, that hadn't been my original outlook. First there had been heartbreak, then rage, then sadness, followed by all the other stages of grief. I'd finally reached acceptance that my marriage was over. Or more to the point, that I'd be starting over at thirty-five years old, a truth that was a serious blow to my pride.

As if that whole ordeal wasn't bad enough, my ex, Oliver, hadn't been as quick to that realization as I had, choosing, instead, to drag this whole painful process out longer than necessary.

Now my divorce was finalized and it felt like I'd just gone through one of the hardest battles of my life, barely managing to come out on the other side. I felt like I'd been beaten down, but I was currently trying my hardest to pick myself up, dust myself off, and start over.

I was a gross, grimy mess by the time my tire was changed and my car re-loaded, and all I could think about as I climbed back into the driver's seat was how badly I needed a drink. And a shower. The shower first, then the drink—or drinks. I deserved more than one, if I did say so myself.

It took another half hour to reach my destination, but the second I pulled into the driveway I felt the tension lessen. My shoulders began to lower from where they'd been raised around my ears since that damn tire popped, and I took my first full breath in far too long.

The front door opened and a petite woman with long

copper hair came charging out as I killed the ignition and pushed my car door open, a huge smile stretched across her pretty face. "Yay! You're here!" she declared loudly, throwing her arms in the air. I barely had time to stand to my full height before she was leaping toward me and wrapping me in a hug, tight enough to pop a lung. The top of her head only reached my chin, but for such a short thing, she was surprisingly strong.

I let out a bewildered laugh, momentarily caught off guard. "Uh . . . hi."

She pulled back, her cheeks flushed and a sheepish smile on her face. "Sorry. I tend to be a little excitable at times." She took a step back and extended her hand to me. "Hi. I'm Iris. But you probably already figured that out. Or at least I hope you did, because if not, this whole thing just got a whole lot creepier."

I brushed her hand aside and pulled her into another embrace. "Nah. You had the right idea the first time. It's so nice to finally meet you in person."

I'd been talking to Iris over the phone and through email and text for weeks now. Buying a house from hundreds of miles away should have been an incredibly stressful process, but Iris had gone above and beyond to make the whole process painless. She'd been a lifesaver through the entire thing, something I appreciated more than she could have possibly understood. Given what a disaster the rest of my life had been recently, it was nice to have one thing go right. And that was all thanks to her.

"Same. It's crazy, but we've spoken so often that I feel like we've known each other forever."

"I know what you mean." The rest of the tension I'd been carrying melted from my bones and muscles as I looked at my new home for the first time ever in person. My lips curled up in a smile as I took it all in. "Wow. It's even better than I thought. The pictures and digital tour didn't really do this place justice."

"It really is a great place." Iris stood beside me, spinning around to grin up at my house. "I almost feel like it was meant to be. Kismet, you know?"

She had a point there. The previous owners had renovated the entire place less than two years earlier, then ended up having to sell when the husband's job moved them out of state. It was only a few days after this place was put on the market that a quick Google search for realtors in the area gave me Iris's name. I reached out to her, specifying that I was hoping I could find something fast. I really didn't want to move into an apartment just to have to repack and do it all again a few months later when I finally found a house, and I didn't want to flush cash down the drain by staying at a hotel for an extended period of time. Not that I'd seen a single hotel as I drove through town. The closest thing was a *motel* that looked like it had been built some time in the fifties and hadn't been renovated since the eighties.

It was like Iris said, kismet. Things just seemed to line up how they were supposed to, and as I stood in my well-maintained front yard looking up at my adorable little bungalow, I felt like I made the right call.

After months of my life being thrown off-kilter, I was finally starting to feel I was where I was meant to be.

Iris glanced at my car, a tiny frown tugging her brows into a V. She lifted her hand to shield her eyes from the sun as she turned to look down the street I'd just driven up. "Is the moving truck coming later?"

"Nope." I held my arms out toward my SUV. "This is it."

"This is . . ." She blinked slowly and shook her head before pasting that smile back onto her face. "Well, okay then. Let's get you unloaded."

It took a second for her words to register. I wasn't used to people being so, well, *nice*. And how sad was it that thanks to all the dickheads out there being loud and proud, a little bit of kindness was enough to throw a person off.

"Oh, no. You don't have to do that. Really. I'm sure you need to get back to work."

She was shaking her head before I even finished my sentence. "Nope. I cleared my schedule so I could be on hand to help if you needed it."

My mouth dropped open in shock. "You—Wow, Iris, that's so sweet. You didn't have to do that."

She lifted a single shoulder. "What can I say? I'm a full-service realtor."

My head fell back on a laugh. "Iris, I think you and I are going to become very good friends."

TWO

LENNON

WITH IRIS'S HELP, it took no time at all to unload all my stuff. Of course, it helped that I didn't technically have much of anything to unpack since I didn't have any furniture yet.

That was something I planned on taking care of as soon as I settled into my new town. I just hadn't been able to bring myself to take anything from my old life with me. Oliver had objected on more than one occasion, but I'd insisted on walking away from pretty much anything I hadn't come into the marriage with. If I was determined to be done with him, I needed a clean slate. After all, by refusing to split things down the middle and letting him have most of it, I'd walked away with a hefty enough settlement that I was able to buy my cute new house as well as afford to furnish it with new pieces that weren't tainted by betrayal. An idea that seriously appealed to me.

When I'd asked Iris earlier the best place to grab a drink, her whole face had lit up. She'd insisted on taking me to her favorite bar, so after a steamy shower to wash off the dirt and grime from having to change my tire, I'd made an effort to make myself presentable, putting on makeup and styling my hair for the first time in weeks. I'd even rummaged through my suitcases for the right outfit instead of just throwing on a pair or leggings or baggy jeans like I'd been doing lately.

I was determined to pull myself out of the post-divorce funk I'd been in, which wasn't all that different from the pre-divorce funk I'd been wallowing in for months. I was starting over. I was a whole new Lennon, and it was high time I started acting like it.

It had done wonders for my self-esteem when Iris swung back around earlier to pick me up and shot me a wolf whistle the moment I stepped out of the house. I'd grinned wide enough to show all my teeth and struck a pose right there in the middle of my front yard as she cat-called me from her car loud enough to put every construction worker in the world to shame.

Now we were sitting at a table in her favorite bar, Toni's Tavern. I was two beers in, and given that I hadn't been much of a drinker in recent years, I was already feeling that pleasant warmth that came with a slight buzz as it slowly traveled through my veins like warm honey.

I brought the amber bottle to my lips and swallowed as I took in the tavern's décor. The walls were covered with old license plates from all over, neon beer signs, and framed sepia-toned prints of vintage motorcycles. Sure, the floors were a little sticky and the air held the faint scent of stale beer and cigarette smoke, but I had to admit, I was pleasantly surprised.

"You know, this place is pretty cool."

Iris sipped her margarita through the tiny cocktail straw as she let her gaze wander. Her cheeks had taken on a bright pink hue as she drank, leading me to believe she was probably as much of a lightweight as I was. "Yeah. Ashland isn't lacking in bars, that's for sure, but Toni's is my favorite."

I tilted my chin toward the large, framed prints. "I'm sensing a bit of a theme with all the motorcycle stuff. I think I counted at least ten on the road today as I drove through town."

She lifted her shoulders, her body bouncing every-so-slightly on her stool to the beat of the music pouring from the jukebox resting against the back wall. "Oh yeah. You're going to be seeing a lot of that around here. A *lot*."

"I'm not really used to seeing so many in the city. Or hearing them." I leaned in closer, lowering my voice. "They're really loud, aren't they?"

She let out a giggle. "I know what you mean. Sometimes, when there are a lot of them in a group, the ground feels like its vibrating." She sucked back more of her margarita. "If you don't mind me asking, what brought you here from the city, anyway?"

I brought the bottle to my lips and drank deeply, draining my beer in three large gulps. That happy little buzz I'd been feeling was quickly fading away, so I spun on my stool, looking around the quickly growing crowd filling the bar for a waitress. The moment I spotted her, I waved my empty bottle in the air, silently requesting another.

Clearing my throat, I turned back to face Iris and rested my elbows on the table. "Well, the short story is that I got divorced."

Her mouth pulled into a wince. "I'm so sorry."

The waitress popped up beside us and deposited our next round on the table in front of us with quick efficiency before disappearing once more. I snatched up the bottle and guzzled so fast I nearly choked on it. I coughed, clearing my lungs before shaking my head. "No, it's fine. It's for the best, believe me."

Her eyes widened. "Sounds like the long version of your short story is pretty intense."

I snorted into my beer. "If you call finding out my husband had been unfaithful practically the entire time we were married intense, then yep."

She choked on her drink and coughed violently. "The *entire* time?"

I nodded vehemently, my head starting to feel nice and floaty. With it, my tongue was getting looser.

"There were some random women sprinkled in throughout our marriage, but the real punch to the ovaries had been the fact he was sleeping with one of my best friends." I could still feel that burn of betrayal that started deep in my belly when I caught them together and singed its way up my throat until I was certain I was going to be sick. Being cheated on hurt no matter what, but the fact it was two people I trusted just made it so much worse.

"She'd been my bridesmaid. She insisted on hosting my bridal shower, for Christ's sake." A derisive snort blew past my nostrils. "She went all out with that party, man. I felt so special that day. I mean, the woman went so far as freezing the heads of roses in balls of ice just so the champagne bucket looked pretty. Who does that?"

"A sociopath," Iris stated with such dry seriousness I couldn't help but giggle in response.

"Right? I mean, who has the time for something like that?"

Her expression turned sympathetic. "So they were carrying on a relationship behind your back?"

I shook my head and drank more, my filter having fallen off at some point as the contents of my third beer bottle got lower and lower. "That's probably the most twisted part of the whole thing. My ex said he didn't have any feelings for her at all, it was just sex."

"*What?*" Iris cried out, slamming her drink down on the table as she leaned in even closer. "They were screwing around behind your back, and he didn't even *like the woman*?"

I shrugged, still unable to wrap my head around it myself, even after all this time. "He said the only reason he ever did it was because he was able to do things in bed with those women that he couldn't do with me." My top lip curled up as I recalled the desperate, pleading look in Oliver's eyes as he begged me to understand.

Iris's head bobbed up and down. "Ah, it's that whole Madonna-whore thing."

My brows pulled down in the center. "Wait, what? What's Madonna got to do with anything?"

"Not Madonna the singer," she said with a laugh. "It's a psychological thing where the guy puts one woman on a pedestal. He thinks of her as this pure, virtuous thing that he doesn't want to defile, so he finds himself the whore he can do all those dirty, depraved things with." She brought the straw to her lips and drank deeply before explaining, "They talked about it on one of the true-crime podcasts I listen to. I'm a bit of a true-crime junkie."

I sipped my beer as I let her words marinate. It made

sense now that I thought about it. As soon as I'd uttered the word divorce, Oliver had lost his ever-loving mind. The hours and hours of crying and begging, the constant phone calls and barrage of text messages had been such a contrast for a man who'd spent the vast majority of our marriage with his dick in some woman that wasn't me.

Not that it had mattered. The moment I found out the truth, it was done. We were over, and there was no putting back together what he'd broken.

"I don't want to be someone's Madonna," I admitted. "I don't want to be put on a pedestal. I want . . . I want passion. I want something wild and crazy."

It was as if Iris had opened my eyes to the truth of my marriage, and now I was seeing everything so clearly. One of the reasons Oliver's infidelity had been so shocking was because he'd spent the years we were together doting on me. Those rose-colored glasses had been so firmly in place that I'd really let myself believe that we had the perfect marriage. But looking back now, I could see all the cracks in the foundation.

That loving, doting man was all surface. There hadn't been anything of substance behind it. There actually hadn't been anything of substance behind our entire relationship. He played the part of the loving husband by buying me spa days and expensive jewelry, using all that flash to blind me to the fact that we never really communicated. Especially about the things that mattered. We spent most of our time doing our own thing, separate from one another, but I let myself believe that was okay, because when we finally did come together, he'd be this tender, affectionate man who seemed like he couldn't get enough of me.

God, what a joke.

The more I thought about it, the angrier I was getting, because the bitter, ugly truth—the truth I'd been denying for so many years—was that our sex life had been *boring*. It wasn't the quantity that was the issue, so much as the quality. That was what was pissing me off, because those other women got what I'd been craving for so long.

The irony was that I'd actually considered finding a couple's therapist, someone who could help me find a way to broach the subject with my husband that things in the bedroom had gotten stale, and I was desperately looking to spice things up.

Turned out it wasn't necessary. He knew how to do it, he just hadn't wanted to do it with *me*.

"You know, I totally changed who I was for him," I confessed bitterly, the words leaving an acrid taste in my mouth as they dripped off the tip of my tongue. "You wouldn't have even reacognized me. I used to be fun and spontaneous, but Oliver was this straight-laced guy from one of those country club families. You know the type." Iris nodded in understanding but remained silent, like she understood I needed to get this all out, purge the ugliness so I could officially start over. "I went to school to be a teacher, but everyone in Oliver's family worked for his dad's company, so I did too. It was expected of me, so I just did it. I didn't want to be a receptionist," I hissed, my face pinched in disgust. "I was meant to be a teacher. But I changed *everything* for him." I gulped back more beer, barely tasting it now. "If he'd wanted something a little kinky in bed, I would have done that. No problem!" I leaned forward and lowered my voice, even though I was well past the point of being able to gage how loud I was being. "Our sex life was boring as hell," I said, a bubble of laughter escaping after that confession. "How is that for irony? He went somewhere else because he didn't want to *defile* me, or whatever," I said, using air quotes around the word defile, "meanwhile, I was so bored I nearly fell asleep with him inside me. More than once!"

Awareness of my surroundings suddenly came rushing back to me. While I already knew I liked Iris, the fact was, we'd only met a handful of hours ago. I was a relative stranger who'd just dropped a rather intimate bomb on her in a very public place. "Did I say too much? I'm sorry. My filter gets a little shaky when I drink. Mainly because I never do. Another change I made when I got with that bastard, Oliver," I tacked on sourly.

Iris burst out laughing, her deep copper hair falling in fiery waves down her shoulders as she threw her head back. "Don't apologize. I actually kind of love it. I can't remember the last time I had this much fun."

That made two of us. I'd spent so many years doing everything in my power to be the perfect little wife that I'd lost sight of myself, and as I guzzled back the rest of my third beer and flagged the waitress down for another, I made a silent oath that I was going to do everything in my power to get her back.

"You know what this moment calls for?" she asked as she waved the waitress down. "Shots!"

I could hear the voice of the Lennon who had been married to Oliver for the past several years in the back of my head telling me shots was a terrible idea, but I was done listening to her. As the waitress sat a couple tequila shooters down on our table, I stuffed a gag in that voice's mouth and slapped a piece of duct tape over it for good measure.

Iris held her shot glass in the air. "To the new Lennon coming out to play."

"To the *old* Lennon returning from the grave," I amended, clinking my glass against hers. "To doing something a little reckless and irresponsible and finding herself again."

"Cheers to that."

We clinked once more and threw the liquor back.

To new beginnings.

THREE

LENNON

"ARE you sure you don't want me to stay with you?"

I shook my head, assuring Iris for the hundredth time I was totally fine hanging around Toni's by myself for a bit longer. We'd been here for a good few hours now—just long enough for me to work up a really nice buzz without crossing a line I was sure I'd regret in the morning. However, Iris had switched to water some time ago and started to yawn uncontrollably half an hour earlier. It was clear she'd hit her wall, and as much as I appreciated her offering to stick it out for me, I wasn't going to make her stay only to keep me company and risk falling asleep on her barstool.

"You're sweet, but it's fine. Go," I insisted.

She gave me a look like she wasn't totally convinced. I was the new girl in town, after all. I hadn't even been in

Ashland for twenty-four hours, but I wasn't going to let that stop me from having a little—or a lot—of fun.

"You're *sure*?" she stressed.

"Positive," I said on a laugh. "I'll get an Uber when I'm ready to head home. No big deal." I wasn't ready to go home yet anyway, especially not after the pep talk I'd given myself earlier. I'd had a blast hanging out with my new friend, but I'd yet to do anything wild and crazy, and I would have been so disappointed in myself if I left this bar without at least grabbing hold of a little piece of that woman I'd once been.

Iris pulled me into a hug that was surprisingly strong for such a tiny woman. "Okay, I'm going." She took a hesitant step back. "But if you change your mind or just want a ride, you call me, okay?"

She really was a good person, so much better than those country club snobs and trust fund brats I used to associate with, and I hoped our friendship continued to grow from here. "I appreciate that, babe, but I'm good."

She let out a huff, finally giving up the fight. "Fine. But at least text me later so I know you made it home okay."

"You got it," I assured her with a big smile. "Now get out of here before you fall asleep where you're standing."

With one last hug, Iris headed out and I hopped back onto my barstool, lifting my beer to my lips and taking a slow, steady sip as I let my gaze wander through the bar. I'd slowed down over the past hour, alternating between beer and water to keep myself hydrated. I wanted to have a fun night, not get so drunk I didn't remember anything that happened. The longer we'd been there, the busier it had gotten. The crowd had thickened, creating a hum of electricity in the air that made me feel more alive than I had in a while.

The music had gotten louder and as the alcohol flowed, the small dancefloor had become packed. People in different stages of drunk filled the bar, and I couldn't help but notice how different this place was from the bars and clubs back in the city. There was a whole lot of denim, and the leather I'd spotted seemed to be worn more for function than fashion. If I had to guess, there wasn't a single designer label in the whole building.

This crowd was way rougher around the edges than what I was used to. There wasn't a golf or polo shirt in sight. The men here seemed to favor dusty motorcycle or cowboy boots over shiny dress shoes or name brand sneakers they wouldn't dare get dirty. The women's skirts were short, their jeans tight, and there was no shortage of cleavage.

This was a biker town, all right, and it made for some very interesting people-watching.

A shift in the atmosphere drew my attention. From the corner of my eye I caught movement at the front of the bar and turned to look as the door was thrown open and a group of men came walking in. Even though the music was still blasting, it was as if the whole place went quiet. A hush moved over the crowd as people turned to watch the men who had just arrived.

It was strange, the power a group of people seemed to have over an entire bar, but there was no missing the stares and whispers and rumbled words spoken under people's breaths.

It only lasted a few seconds, then everybody went back to what they were doing, but it was enough to leave an impression on me. Whoever these guys were, they were renowned. I just wasn't sure if that was for a good reason or not.

I was vaguely aware that other people started in their direction, men coming in for handshakes and backslaps, women who were much more blatant, pressing themselves up against the guys in ways that left no question as to what they were looking for. But I hadn't had a chance to take in all of them, because moments after they snagged a table a few yards away from my own, my attention snared on one man in particular, and the moment I locked in, I couldn't force myself to look away.

He was the complete opposite of my ex-husband in every single way. At least a week's worth of light stubble coated a strong, square jaw that looked like it could have been carved from granite and surrounded a sinful mouth. He had nice, full lips, the bottom one just a tad puffier, but the top lip had the perfect cupid's bow. His dirty blond hair was overly long, hanging past his ears and curling at the ends near the collar of his shirt.

There was the slightest bump in the otherwise straight line of his nose, leading me to believe it had been broken a time or two but still managed to set in a way that didn't come close to detracting from his looks. Heavy brows rested over eyes that were such a dark brown they looked like pools of oil from where I sat. His plain tee stretched across a broad chest and hugged defined biceps, and long, thick thighs were encased in faded denim that led down to yet another pair of worn-in motorcycle boots.

On top of looking like the kind of man who rolled out of bed and dressed in the first thing he touched—a look that *absolutely* worked for him, by the way—he also looked like the kind of guy who'd be more inclined to beat a person with a golf club than use it for what it was actually meant for. In other words, he'd have a man like Oliver pissing his pressed khakis with a single look.

He moved through the bar like a panther, somehow graceful, but with an unmistakable power beneath that was almost menacing. This man would never be mistaken for prey. Wherever he was, whoever he was with, he was the predator, and anyone who made the mistake of thinking otherwise would quickly learn their lesson.

He was dangerous. There was no doubt about that. But he was also the sexiest man I'd ever set my eyes on.

I wasn't sure if it was the beers I'd consumed or the fact that my sorry excuse of a sex life had been at the forefront of my thoughts after my talk with Iris, but my body was suddenly reacting in a way it never had before, all from a simple look at a guy across a crowded bar. It was like it had suddenly shot awake after hibernating for the past seven years. It was nearly enough to steal my breath and had me squirming on my stool as I raked my gaze over the man unabashedly.

The guy's head turned in my direction, those inky black eyes landing square on me, and all of a sudden it felt like the temperature in the room had gone up ten degrees. Heat crawled up my chest and neck as I brought my beer to my lips and drank, my mouth having gone dry as the Sahara.

Then he smiled, all straight white teeth and sexy, full lips, and *damn*! What a smile it was. The impact of it was so strong that even with half the bar between us, it slammed into me hard enough it was a miracle I hadn't been thrown right off my stool.

Even though I'd been caught ogling, I couldn't bring myself to look away. Those dark, oil-slick eyes of his glinted as he shot me a wink, and from behind the mouth of my beer bottle I felt my lips curling up in return.

A voice in the back of my head shouted out just then: *Here's your wild and crazy, Lennon. What are you going to do about it?*

I'd been out of the game for so long that I would have been lying if I said I wasn't intimidated or anxious about what the hell I was supposed to do next. My instincts screamed at me to break eye contact, to duck my head and hide behind the curtain of my hair, but I shoved that feeling down and forced my head to stay up as I thought back to how I used to let a guy know I was interested before Oliver and I got together.

Lowering my bottle to the table, I peeked the tip of my tongue out and swiped it across my bottom lip before smiling at the guy and batting my lashes just enough to not look ridiculous. Or at least that was what I hoped.

This had been so much easier when I was younger and out with my girlfriends. At least then they'd tell me whether or not I was making a fool of myself.

I let out a slow breath of relief when, instead of turning his back on me or giving me a look like I'd just totally weirded him out, he leaned over to say something to one of his buddies before grabbing the beer bottle that had just been placed in front of him and heading in my direction.

The crowd parted, everyone jumping out of the way

to give him plenty of room as he moved toward me. A man like him didn't swagger, there was something about him that was too volatile for that, the danger I'd sensed creeping right below the surface. But that didn't mean he wasn't sexy as hell as he moved, and the closer he got, the more I noticed the dude was even bigger than I'd originally thought, standing a good half foot taller than me. If I had to guess, he was at least six three, and as he came to a stop at my table, I realized every powerful inch of him was packed with muscle.

Yeah, this guy was most definitely going to be my crazy, reckless adventure. *For damn sure.*

I'd never had a one-night stand before. Until that very moment, I hadn't thought I was a one-night-stand kind of woman, but as I tried my best to take all of the guy in as discreetly as possible, there was a spark in my veins I'd never felt before. Certainly not where Oliver was concerned.

After the epic shit-show that was my divorce, the last thing on earth I wanted was another relationship, especially when I'd barely finished picking up the tattered pieces of my life and started over.

But one night of fun couldn't possibly hurt, right? And this dude looked like he knew how to have a *lot* of fun.

"Hey." His voice came out rough and gritty, a low rasp, like his words were sandpaper, that matched the guy perfectly and made my belly swoop with just that one word.

My smile widened. *Looks like I still got it*, I thought. That was a relief. "Hi."

"No way in hell I'd ever forget a face like yours, so the fact I don't recognize you means you must be new in town or you're just passing through."

I took another sip, using the beer to tamp down the giddiness fluttering inside me. I liked this guy's style. He jumped right in, cutting out all the awkward small talk. I could appreciate that.

"I actually just moved here today. Got everything unloaded at my new place and was in desperate need of a drink, so here I am. I'm Lennon, by the way."

Those inky black pools scanned down my body appreciatively, taking in everything he could see from the table up, and from the way the corner of his mouth hooked upward in a delectable smirk, he liked what he was seeing.

Well, the feeling's mutual, buddy.

"Dig the name, sweetheart. I'm Pope."

My eyebrow rose on my forehead. "Your name is really Pope?"

A deep, low chuckle rumbled in his chest. "You're one to talk. Lennon? Haven't heard that a lot."

My shoulders shook with silent laughter. "Blame it on my Mom. Apparently she was a huge Beatles fan."

"It's a cool-ass name. And Pope's actually my last name. First name's Courtland, but nobody calls me that, mainly because I'd beat the hell out of anyone who'd call me Courtland."

I giggled, my smile widening. "Courtland's not such a bad name. You could go by Court," I suggested. "That's kind of cool."

"My dad's Court. I'm named after him."

I nodded, pulling my bottom lip between my teeth and giving it a nervous nip. "Well, I like Pope. It"—I did a full body scan of the guy, not caring in the slightest that I was being so obvious—"fits you. Kind of badass."

Pope braced his forearms on the table, leaning in closer. He smelled like leather and wind mixed with just the perfect amount of musk and something spicy. He lowered his voice, the rich timbre vibrated close to my ear, causing goosebumps to spread across my skin. "Well, cool-ass Lennon. I think to celebrate your move to town and my luck at meeting you on your very first night, you should let me buy your next round. What's your poison?"

I'd been alternating between beer and water, but something about this guy made me want to throw caution to the wind. If I was really going to do this, let old Lennon out of her cage after being locked up for so long, I was going full tilt.

"Tequila."

He nodded, the glint in his eyes telling me he approved of my choice. He lifted his big hand in the air, flagging down a waitress. "Four shots of Don Julio on my tab, sweetheart. Thanks."

"You got it, Pope. Anything else?"

He jerked his head toward my half-empty bottle. "Another beer for her."

So much for not waking up hating life tomorrow, but I had a feeling I was going to need a bit of liquid courage, so I didn't make a fuss.

She nodded and hustled off to fill his order, leaving him to turn his focus back to me. It was a deep, penetrating stare that I could so easily get lost in.

"Thanks for the drinks."

"My pleasure, babe. It's what we do here. We're hospitable like that."

"Good to know."

The waitress came back a minute later and deposited our drinks on the table. I grabbed one of the glasses when Pope did, mirroring his actions as he lifted it in a toast. "To your first night in town."

"And to having some fun." I clinked my glass against his and threw the shot back, ready to officially get this night started.

FOUR

LENNON

THE DOOR CRASHED against the wall as we slammed through it, our movements as frantic and messy as our lips were as we kissed each other with a level of desperation I'd never experienced before. We stumbled out of the bar with staggered steps, neither of us wanting to break away from the other now that the game had officially started.

Pope's hands traveled down my body as I raked my fingers in his long, silky hair, tangling it in my fingers to keep him from pulling away. Our kiss was sloppy and fueled by hunger, but it was still the best kiss I'd ever experienced, hands down, and no way was I ready for it to end.

Fortunately, Pope seemed to be on board. Instead of breaking away, his large hand molded to the cheeks of my ass over my jeans and squeezed hard before hoisting me up.

My legs locked around his trim hips, my hair flying wild as he spun us around. A moment later, my back collided with the exterior of the building. The rough, jagged surface of the brick scratched at my skin through the material of my top, but the sharp abrasions only amplified the lust I was currently drowning in. I'd had so many years of boring, vanilla sex that didn't even end in an orgasm most of the time, that I'd all but forgotten what I liked in the bedroom. But as Pope manhandled me, feasting from my mouth as he rocked his pelvis between my thighs, that long, steel length behind his fly rubbing against me in the most tantalizing way, I suddenly remembered I liked it *rough*.

"Jesus," he grunted against my mouth before pulling away in order to drag his teeth down that sensitive column of my neck. "You're fucking wild, Raven."

He'd taken to calling me Raven about an hour into our meeting, using the word for the first time as he reached out and fingered the long, loose strands of my black hair. I'd loved the way my name rolled off his tongue when he said it, but having him call me Raven was just as hot. I'd never had a nickname before. Oliver had always stuck to the basics: baby or babe or honey with a whole lot of sweetheart and sweetie mixed in there. Nothing with any imagination.

I moaned as I rolled my hips, rubbing against his hard-on as the barrage of sensations I was experiencing in that moment continued to roll through me. We were basically dry humping against the wall, and I felt closer to a release than I ever had with Oliver.

Fisting his hair, I gave his head a tug, forcing it back so I could pull his bottom lip between my teeth and bite down sharply, showing him exactly how wild I was feeling.

My nipples were hard enough to cut glass and my panties were soaked through. I was so into him and what we were doing that everything else had ceased to exist. We were in the middle of a crowded parking lot, tearing at each other where anyone could see, and I didn't care. Not one damn bit.

He hissed at my stinging nip, pulling back just enough to blink up at me, and I could see from the way his dark eyes flashed beneath the harsh exterior lights and the way his dick twitched between us that he got off on that bite of pain in a really big way. "Oh, you have no idea," I told him, my voice low and throaty with need.

A primal growl rumbled up his throat, the vibrations of it penetrating my chest and sending another flood of arousal between my thighs. In the blink of an eye, we were moving again, the brisk air floating across my skin and my hair whipping me in the face as he spun us around again. This time my back collided with the cold, hard metal of the hood of a car.

"Oh!" I cried at the chill seeping into my skin, but before it could really penetrate, Pope was back on me, his mouth even more ravenous. One hand on my hip kept me in place while he slid the other one up my outer thigh, hooking around the back of my knee, pushing it closer to my chest and open wider.

The fog I was in only partially lifted, just enough for me to tilt my head back and look at the car I was currently spread out across. "W-whose car is this?"

"Don't give a fuck."

Well, if he didn't care, I sure as hell wasn't going to worry about it either.

"Fuck. *Fuck!*" he clipped as his mouth moved along the skin of my neck and across my collarbones. With how rough he was being, I was sure I'd have marks the following morning, but that only turned me on more. I *wanted* this wild, beautiful, feral man to mark me. To use my body in any way he saw fit. "Need to feel you right fucking now, Raven. I can't wait."

His level of desperation matched my own. It had nothing to do with the amount of alcohol I'd consumed tonight and everything to do with *him*, but all my inhibitions were long gone, having flown out the window sometime between that first shot we shared and him asking me if I wanted to get out of there.

I blinked, taking Pope in and feeling a shiver travel through my whole body at the power boiling just beneath the surface. God, had I ever been with a man so . . . massive? The answer to that was a resounding no.

"Then don't," I panted.

He smiled then, the way his lips curled back from his teeth making him look downright ferocious, like he wanted to eat me alive in that very moment. And, *god*, but I wanted that too.

He leaned in, his large frame blocking out the silvery moonlight as he hovered over me. His hand moved to the waistband of my jeans, his deft fingers making quick work of popping the button and lowering the zipper.

"Dig those sexy fingers back in my hair and hold on tight, baby."

As soon as my fingers tangled in those long, silky locks, his hand moved, diving down the front of my pants and cupping me between my thighs. I sucked in a sharp gasp, my neck and back arching off the cool metal of the car's hood as he swiped his finger through my slit, homing in on my clit.

"Pope." I moaned his name, the sound turning into a whimper as he circled my clit with the perfect amount of pressure.

"Jesus Christ," he grunted, his tongue coming out to swipe across his bottom lip. "You're drenched for me already."

My body writhed, the metal beneath me groaning and creaking as I circled my hips, chasing his touch so I could get those long, thick fingers right where I wanted them.

He chuckled, deep and rich and sinful while reaching up with his free hand to pluck my distended nipple through the material of my shirt and the flimsy lace of my bra. "Look at you squirm. You got a greedy cunt, don't you, baby?"

"I-I need—"

"Say it," he ordered gruffly. "You want me to give it to you, you gotta say it."

"I need more," I pleaded. My brain had short-circuited, and I was having trouble forming words. I was *right there,* on the cusp of a climax that threatened to throw me over the edge, but what he was doing wasn't quite enough. And from the arrogant smirk that toyed at the corners of his sinful mouth, he knew it.

"More what, Raven?"

At his pushing, something inside me snapped. I'd spent too many years of my life unsatisfied, and I was done. I knew what I wanted, damn it, and I was deter-mined to get it. I was done being unfulfilled. A soft growl worked its way up my throat. I tightened my hold on Pope's hair and yanked his face closer to mine as I bared my teeth. "I want you to fuck me with those long fingers of yours. I want you to be rough with me. Make me come right here on this car."

"Fuck yeah, baby. Knew you were the kind of woman who'd rock my goddamn world."

He was one to talk, because I felt like my world was spinning like a top. His hand shifted and all the air expelled from my lungs as he speared me with two fingers, slamming them deep inside me like I'd wanted.

"*Yes*," I moaned, throwing my head back, my back arching so deep I felt like I was folding in half.

"Christ, you're tight," Pope gritted as he pulled his fingers out before plunging them back in. Even with my clothes restricting him, he'd managed to give it to me as hard as I demanded. With each upward stroke, those long digits slid across a place inside me that made stars burst before my eyes. I'd never been touched like this in my life. Oliver wouldn't have been able to find my G-spot if he had a map, flashlight, and a big neon arrow pointing right at it, meanwhile, it took Pope two seconds to figure out how and where to touch me to have me crying out into the night. "Jesus, your pussy's squeezing the shit out of my fingers, baby. Bet you're gonna feel like a vise wrapped around my cock."

His hand at my breast squeezed, pinching my nipple hard enough to send a bolt of lightning straight to my core.

A rush of wetness drenched his fingers, making him

groan. "Pope," I whimpered, my release coming on strong and fast, like a tidal wave seconds away from reaching land and devastating everything. My fingers in his hair clenched even tighter, pulling his face closer to mine. "I'm close. God, I'm so fucking close."

"Fuck yes. Give it to me, Raven. Right fucking now."

I tumbled right over that edge into the abyss. If not for Pope slamming his lips down on mine in a ravenous kiss, my screams would have been enough to bring everyone around the corner, giving them one hell of a show. Wave after wave crashed into me and Pope continued working between my thighs, his fingers continuing to stroke until there was nothing left. He swallowed down every sound I made, only stopping once my body went boneless.

I sucked in deep, heaping inhales, trying to catch my breath as I peeled my eyes open to take in the gratified smirk stretching across Pope's face. My chest heaved with each strained breath. "That was . . . *Damn.*" It was all I could think to say, because the man had just annihilated every brain cell I had.

He chuckled, slowly pulling his hand from the front of my pants. I'd just had the best orgasm of my entire freaking life, but a renewed feeling of lust swept over me as I watched Pope suck those fingers into his mouth, licking them clean of my arousal.

His black eyes flashed with hunger. "Tastes fucking

incredible," he grunted, then his hand shot out toward me. His fingers wrapped around the front of my throat, and he used his grip to yank me up to sitting before crashing his lips against mine.

I returned the kiss as soon as his tongue plunged into my mouth, moaning at the taste of me mingling with the beer and tequila he drank earlier.

He pulled away a few seconds later, his gaze hazy with need as he stared down at me. "You ever been on the back of a bike before, Raven?"

I shook my head, licking my swollen lips.

His curved up in a smirk that made my belly swoosh. "Then tonight's your lucky night. Because the fun's just getting started."

FIVE

LENNON

THE POUNDING in my skull beat in time with the pulsing throb between my thighs as I blinked my scratchy eyes open. The backs of my lids were like sandpaper against my eyeballs as I tried to bring my cloudy vision into focus.

A ceiling came into view, the fan hanging in the center swirling in slow, lazy circles, just enough to keep the air in the room circulating. Speaking of rooms—I took in the dark navy walls I didn't recognize, trying to figure out where the hell I was. I lay frozen for several seconds, holding my breath as consciousness slowly crept back in, digging through the mire in my brain in an effort to piece together what was going on.

Then the events of the night before came rushing back at lightning speed.

I sucked in a breath and gave my body a little wiggle

beneath the soft-as-hell covers draped over me. Sure enough, the twinge of pain between my legs was all the proof I needed that my mind hadn't conjured up something completely insane.

Even though I knew what had happened already, I slowly lifted the covers draped over my chest and peeked beneath, just to make absolutely certain.

Yep. Naked as the day I was born. And were those— okay, yeah, I had a handful of bruise-colored hickeys sprinkled across my chest, a few spots that looked like teeth marks on my breasts, as well as several patches of beard burn.

I remembered the beers. And the tequila. *Ugh*, the tequila.

Never again, I silently vowed, though it wasn't the first time I'd sworn that to myself. I'd also claimed *never again* when it came to vodka and red wine, and the three bottles of Cab I'd jacked from Oliver's precious wine collection before moving to Ashland and the bottle of Tito's in my otherwise empty freezer were enough to call me a dirty liar.

A small chuffing snore yanked me back into reality, and I slowly turned my head. Pope lay beside me on his stomach facing in my direction, his light hair fanned out on the pillow beside the one I was resting on. The sun was only starting to rise outside the bedroom window, but it made the room light enough that I could make out his features clearly enough. Even in sleep he looked like a warrior, like he could spring to consciousness at any second, ready to pillage and raid with the rest of the Viking horde at his command.

My skin heated as I slowly pushed to sitting, clutching the sheet to my chest to hide my nakedness, even though there wasn't much point to it. As more and more of the night before played through my muddled brain, I remembered there wasn't a single inch of my body that Pope hadn't gotten extremely up close and personal with.

God, the man had played my body like it was an instrument he'd spent his entire life practicing until he was an expert.

But in the light of day and without the haze of booze lowering my guard, I was suddenly very aware that the man currently asleep beside me was a complete stranger.

I twisted and threw my legs over the side of the mattress, placing my feet on the chilly hardwood floor. Moving as quietly as possible, I hustled around the bedroom in search of my clothes. I found my jeans and top, throwing them on in a hurry, stuffing my bra into my pocket after locating it dangling from the corner of a bedside table.

I found my shoes and purse, scooping them all up and clutching them in my arms as I spun in a circle, trying to locate my underwear.

"Screw it," I whispered to myself and started for the bedroom door, but movement from the bed caught my eye and had me pausing. I looked back over my shoulder as Pope stirred, holding my breath as he turned his head to face the other direction in his sleep. The sheets pooled at his waist, his arms bent at the elbows, his hands shoved beneath his pillow. His smooth skin wrapped around muscles that felt just as hard and powerful as they looked—something I knew from experience.

Intricately designed tattoos ran from his large, broad shoulders all the way down to his hands and fingers. There was more ink etched along his ribs, but the one tattoo that caught and held my attention most was the massive piece that took up the majority of his wide, ripped back, from the base of his neck nearly all the way down to those sexy dimples right above his tight, firm ass.

The tattoo was a work of art, no other way to describe it. It was the Grim Reaper, his face an angry skull beneath his hood. He held his scythe in one bony hand while the other clutched the handlebar of the motorcycle he was riding. Beneath the design in thick black letters were the words *Ride or Die*. Just like the man, the tattoo was menacing and beautiful at the same time—two things I hadn't thought could possibly go together.

He really was incredible. Every single inch of him. And he'd popped up at just the right moment, giving me a night I'd never forget. In all the shit that had been swirling around in my life recently, he'd been a single bright spot, a memory I would hold on to and cherish for years to come.

I appreciated our night together more than he'd ever know; my wild and crazy choice that I'd made just for me.

But it was time to tuck that reckless part of me away again. I'd have to remember to let her out more than once every several years.

Creeping out of the bedroom, I pulled the door closed behind me and padded down the hall. We'd been so desperate for each other the night before that there hadn't been time to really take in Pope's place. The living room was full of masculine furniture that had to have cost a pretty penny, the rich, tobacco colored leather looking soft and buttery. The wood floors were stained a deep espresso that worked really well with the pale cream walls.

There were signs here and there that this was the home of a bachelor, with some clothes tossed around, shoes kicked off in the living room, and a few dishes on the coffee table, but it wasn't a pigsty. Far from it. It was actually a really nice place, and if I'd had time, I probably would have looked around more, but I needed to get out of there before Pope woke up.

I was almost to the front door when I tripped on

something laying on the floor, nearly dropping my purse and shoes as I stumbled.

Bending forward, I scooped up the leather vest that I remembered peeling off Pope's shoulders as we crashed through his front door, tearing at each other's clothes like we couldn't get naked fast enough.

I'd been so enamored with him the night before that I hadn't paid much attention to his clothing choices, but as I held up the vest, I spotted patches sewn into the faded and scuffed material that I hadn't noticed before. There was a patch on the front that read president, and another that sported the same words tattooed on his skin, *Ride or Die.* I flipped it over, seeing that same Grim Reaper on a motorcycle stitched into the leather that covered Pope's entire back, and beneath it read *Iron Wraiths MC, Ashland TN.*

I shook my head in an attempt to clear the tequila fog, and winced as my brain rattle around in my skull. I didn't know what the hell an Iron Wraith was, and I was too damn hungover to try and figure it out.

I draped the vest over the back of the couch, putting it out of my mind as I hustled for the door. As soon as I made it onto the porch, I reached into my purse, fishing around for my phone. There were a handful of unread texts waiting for me; two from Iris asking if I'd made it home safely, and the rest from Oliver, the tone of each just as desperate and pleading as every other message he'd sent me over the past several months.

Oliver: *I miss you so much, it physically hurts.*

Oliver: *Will you please text me back?*

Oliver: *Just let me know you're all right. I'm going out of my mind.*

Oliver: *I still love you.*

Oliver: *They meant nothing. You're it for me.*

Man, he really had a hell of a way of proving that last one. Then, finally . . .

Oliver: *Please, sweetheart, can we just talk?*

I let out a snort and shook my head as I mumbled to myself, "Not fucking likely, asshole."

A smile stretched across my lips as I hit edit on his contact information. I hadn't blocked his number before because I'd been waiting for the divorce to finalize and for my settlement to come through, but now that it had, and I was officially in my new town, there was no reason to keep that last line of communication open. Hitting *Block* on his number then deleting his contact all together was more satisfying than that first sip of coffee in the morning or watching all those adorable panda reels on social media.

With that done, I scrolled through my apps and requested an Uber, letting out a sigh of relief that there just so happened to be a car in the area, less than five minutes away. I moved out to the street so the car wouldn't have to pull into the driveway, just in case the engine was too loud, and as I waited, I turned back to look up at the house I'd all but run away from.

Large glass windows and dark wood made up a home that looked like a cabin that had been modernized to fit today's esthetic. It was a lot bigger than I'd been expecting, nestled back in the mass of trees that surrounded the huge lot, the foothills of the Smoky Mountains rising up behind it. Off to the left and a little up the hill was a large metal building with roll-up doors that were currently closed. It wasn't a garage—the house had one attached to it already—so I assumed it was some sort of shop.

"Wow," I breathed at the beauty that surrounded me. I didn't have the first clue what Pope did for a living— we hadn't really done the whole 'get to know you schtick' before jumping into bed together—but whatever it was, he had to be well off to afford a place like this. None of the houses on the street were small by any stretch of the imagination, and the space between neigh- bor's was at least an acre, massive compared to the tiny strip of grass between my cute little bungalow and my new neighbor's place.

This wasn't some sort of cookie cutter subdivision. No, this was the kind of neighborhood where you had to shell out a pretty penny for the land, then custom build your dream home on the lot. I only knew that because it was what Oliver's parents had wanted to do so badly, and even they couldn't afford something like this.

A dark colored sedan came rolling up the quiet street just then, pulling to a stop in front of me and rolling down the driver's side window.

"You Lennon?"

"Yep. That's me." My cheeks flamed as the guy behind the wheel looked me up and down, his eyebrows creeping higher on his forehead. I hadn't stopped to consider how I looked before now, and I could only imagine what the dude had to be thinking. Ratty hair, last night's makeup most likely smeared around, my shoes dangling from my fingers. I quickly crossed my arms over my chest to try and block the fact that I wasn't wearing my bra on this crisp morning, hoping he hadn't noticed the situation down there yet. It was quite obvious I'd tied a serious one on the night before and was in the midst of an epic walk of shame. However, I couldn't find it in me to be embarrassed. Last night had just been too damn good.

With my head held high, I skipped the last few feet between me and the car and hopped into the back seat. "Thanks for the ride. I know it's kind of early."

The guy's eyes met mine in the rearview mirror just a moment before returning to the road. "No sweat. Fun night?"

"Oh yeah," I said on a giggle. There was no stopping

the grin that split my face in half just then as I recalled all the things Pope had done to me the night before. Hell, there were moves in there that I hadn't even known existed, and after so many orgasm-less years, I'd actually lost count of how many times the dude had gotten me off.

I was *still* riding that endorphin high, and I'd hold onto it for as long as I possibly could.

SIX

LENNON

AS THE CAR pulled away from Pope's house and started down the street, I remembered the messages from Iris still waiting on my phone.

I quickly shot off a text, not wanting to risk waking her by calling.

Me: *Alive and well. Sorry it took so long to get back to you.*

I saw instantly that she read it, and a second later, my phone started ringing.

I swiped to answer, bring the phone to my ear. "Hey."

Her voice came through the line in rapid bursts before I could get another word out. "Oh thank god! You're alive. I've been freaking out all night when I didn't hear from you. I thought you might have been kidnapped or buried alive or locked in a shack in the middle of the woods somewhere!"

I couldn't help but giggle. "Babe, I think you should probably lay off the true crime podcasts for a while."

There was a brief moment of silence before she spoke again. "Yeah, okay. You may have a point."

"Still, I'm sorry I worried you. That wasn't cool."

A heavy sigh of relief blew through the line. "It's okay. I have a habit of jumping to worst case scenarios. My mind can be a crazy place, sometimes. I'm sure you were already in bed or something when I texted you."

I curled my lips between my teeth to keep from laughing as I though, *or something.*

Technically, I'd been stretched out on the hood of some random car when she texted me—at least the first time. Something I still couldn't believe I'd done. Truth was, even with all the risk that had come with being so brazen, I couldn't say I regretted it. There was something thrilling about having a man like Pope be so desperate to touch me he hadn't been able to wait. It made me feel powerful, something I hadn't felt in far too long.

"Um, actually, I'm only just now on my way home," I admitted, a giddy smile pulling at my lips.

"What do you mean, you—*ohhh.*" Then a sharp squeal came through the line, nearly rendering me deaf. "Look at you, getting your freak on already. Talk about being an overachiever. So who was the guy? Oh! Was it that guy in the football jersey that was sitting at the bar? Or the one in the button down that had been playing darts? He was really cute."

"Um, neither," I admitted. "It was just some guy who showed up after you left." Then I remembered the leather vest with the insignia stitched onto the back. "Hey, Iris, what's an Iron Wraith?"

A choking sound came from the front of the car, and when my attention shot to my Uber driver, I could have sworn he was doing his best to fight back a laugh.

"What?"

"Iron Wraith," I repeated. "What—or I guess who— are they?"

"The local motorcycle club?" she asked, her question creating a record scratch in my brain. "How do you know about them?"

"Wait. Motorcycle club? You mean—" I caught the Uber driver's judge-y gaze in the mirror and twisted to face the window, lowering my voice in a lame attempt for some privacy. "Like, *a gang*?" I hissed out in a whisper.

"I don't think they like to be called a gang. And there's no actual proof that they're into anything illegal. At least not that I know of." Her tone seemed far too casual for the words that had just come out of her mouth.

Although, I had to admit that I didn't really know much about any of that beyond the episodes of *Sons of Anarchy* I'd seen. And honestly, I'd been too busy lusting after the main guy on the show to really pay attention to what was happening. All I knew was that while a lot of them were hot as hell, they weren't exactly good guys. "Why are you asking about them anyway?"

"Well, um . . ." I cleared my throat uncomfortably, heat rising up my neck and settling into my cheeks until they felt like they were on fire. "So, the guy's house I'm leaving right now? Well, I think he might be the president of the thing."

She sucked in a gasp so big I worried she might pop a lung. "You *think*?"

"Well, he had a leather vest thingy, and one of the patches stitched on the front said president." I was suddenly hit with an overwhelming sensation of *oh, holy god, what have I done.* I'd been wondering when that feeling would take effect.

"Holy shit," Iris breathed. "You had a one night stand with Courtland Pope?"

My lips parted and the words fell out of my mouth. "Just Pope. He's not real big on people using his first name."

"Oh my god, you did!" Iris shrieked so loudly even the Uber driver winced. "How—what—how did this even happen?"

"I don't know. It just happened," I whisper-yelled defensively before lowering my voice even further and trying to find that blissful calm I'd been experiencing all morning. "You know, I was actually feeling pretty damn good about what went down until this phone call. Now I'm kind of freaking out."

Her tone went from high and shrill to soothing in a single beat. "Don't freak out. It's all good."

That helped a little bit to loosen the knot that had formed in my chest over the past two minutes. "You think?"

"Yeah. But I think there are some things I should explain about this town and the way things run around here. How about I head over to your place with a couple coffees and some donuts?"

My stomach let out an appreciative growl at the thought of food and coffee. "Yeah, okay. That sounds good. Give me thirty?"

"You got it."

I disconnected the call and stowed my phone in my purse, heaving out a sigh and wishing I was still riding that high I'd been on earlier.

I closed my eyes and rested my forehead against the cool window, my hangover returning with force.

"Decisions from the night before look pretty different in the light of day, huh?"

I shot my Uber driver a glare through the mirror.

"That's enough out of you, thank you very much. Unless you want that five star rating of yours to drop drastically."

He lifted a hand to his mouth and mimed locking it shut and tossing away the key.

That's what I thought.

I'd just climbed out of the shower and thrown on a pair of leggings and a slouchy, cropped sweater when my doorbell rang. I had to hand it to Iris, she was punctual, that was for sure. It had been exactly thirty minutes since I hung up with her, and my need for caffeine had steadily grown in that time.

I twisted my damp hair into a bun on the top of my head and secured it with a clip before reaching for the knob and pulling the door open.

"The coffee fairy's here," She declared, holding up a cardboard tray of drinks in one hand and a white bakery box in the other. "I wasn't sure what flavor donuts you liked, so I just got a variety."

I made grabby hands before snatching the box away from her and stepped aside to wave her in. "Perfect. Just so happens that sugar and carbohydrates are my favorite flavors."

She trailed me into the kitchen. "Ah, then I made the right call on the coffee, too." She extended one of the paper cups to me. "Took a chance on a caramel latte with an extra shot." That extra hit of espresso instantly solidified her place as one of my favorite people of all time.

"You're the smartest person I know." I let out a happy sigh and I drank deep, moaning as that first splash of sweetened coffee hit my tongue. "Bless you, woman. You're a lifesaver." I took another gulp of the piping hot nectar of the gods before hopping up onto the counter and patting the cool marble beside me. "I'd offer you somewhere to sit, but I still don't have any furniture. That's on the agenda for today. But feel free to pull up some counter top in the meantime."

She braced her palms on the edge and lifted herself up to sit beside me, swinging her legs back and forth as she flipped open the donut box between us, taking a blueberry cake for herself and passing me a cherry filled glazed. I bit the thing nearly in half, the tartness of the cherry filling combined with the sugar from the glaze, creating the perfect bite. I washed it all down with more coffee as I twisted on the counter to face her, arching a single eyebrow and trying to look as serious as possible for someone who was covered in hickeys and beard burn beneath her clothes.

"I got the impression on the phone earlier that you're holding back something kind of major about this town." I licked a dollop of cherry filling off my thumb before pointing the donut at her. I used my best "stern teacher" voice as I ordered, "Start talking, sister."

"It's not that bad, honestly. More like small town lore," she assured me, but the contrition in her expression made me skeptical. "And I was going to tell you, I swear. I just wanted to give you a chance to settle in and fall in love with the town first."

"Tell me what, exactly?" My mind had started spinning out of control since our earlier call, but in my defense, with the way things had been going lately, I'd learned to expect the worst and be pleasantly surprised when it didn't happen. "Does the town sit on a Hell Mouth or something? Do the residents pick a couple every year to sacrifice for good weather and a healthy crop yield?" I sucked in a breath, my eyes widening in horror. "Please don't tell me there's a pet cemetery somewhere in the mountains, because if so, I'm out. That's a major deal breaker."

Her eyes rounded before she burst into laughter. "If I need to lay off true crime, you need to step away from the scary movies, babe."

She had a point, but still. "Come on, Ris," I said, my voice coming out in a whine. I blamed the hangover that was still holding on. "Just tell me. Is the guy dangerous or something?" I sucked in a sharp gasp. "Oh my god." I slapped a hand over my eyes. "Please tell me I didn't sleep with a felon. That would be just my luck."

Her fingers wrapped around my wrist, pulling my hand away so she could see my face. "Okay, just calm down. You don't have anything to worry about. I might not know those guys very well—I mean, we don't exactly run in the same circles—but the few run-ins I'd had with Pope or his crew, they've always been perfectly nice. There are people who will warn you to stay away from them just because of the fact they're part of a motorcycle club and the stigma that comes with that, but for every one of them, you'll have someone else speaking their praise. It's kind of known around here that if you need help and law enforcement is giving you the run-around, they're your best bet."

My brows furrowed in confusion. "What do you mean?"

She pulled her bottom lip between her teeth and nibbled on it almost nervously. "Well, I guess the best way to explain it is to start from the beginning."

My fingers itched for the bottle of vodka in my freezer to add to my coffee, but I refrained. The last thing I needed after last night was more booze.

"I guess I should start by telling you about the Bradys."

"Who are the Bradys?" I asked around a bite of my

second donut. Seriously, these were little circles of sugary heaven.

Iris's face pinched, a look of contempt twisting up her pretty features. For such a bubbly, happy woman, I hadn't expected her face to be able to pull in such a way, but it was clear just from the look of her just then that she wasn't a fan of these illustrious Bradys, whoever they were.

"They're a family here in Ashland—one of the founding families, actually—they basically run the whole town."

I swallowed down the bite of donut I'd just taken, chasing it with more coffee. "I take it from your tone of voice, you aren't a big fan of the family."

"They're literally the spawns of Satan, Len. *Literally*. You'll quickly discover most people here feel the same way about them that I do." Her hand suddenly shot out and latched onto mine, her fingers wrapping around tightly. "I'm not exaggerating when I tell you that these are bad people, Lennon. You do not want to get mixed up with them."

I shook my head. "I don't understand. If they're so terrible, how is it they run this place like you say."

"How else?" She huffed out a bitter scoff through her nose. "Money. It's always about money. They're loaded, and they just love to hold that over everyone whenever they get the chance. Rudolph Brady started up a local law firm some time in the fifties back when this place was mainly farmland and ranching families, before it had taken off, and let me tell you, that man was crooked as a fishhook. Raised the rest of his family to be the same damn way, and each and every one of them has injected that same poison into their own kids. It's basically generation after generation of spoiled, narcissistic sociopaths with god complexes."

My lips stretched into a long, tight line. "Yikes." I wasn't sure a worse combination existed than the one she'd just described.

"Exactly. So, Rudolph eventually got himself elected as County Judge, and before he retired, he used his money and influence to get his son elected as District Attorney. It's been like that ever since. No one but a Brady has held that position, and any time someone else has tried to run against them, it's turned really ugly for that person."

"Ugly how?" I asked cautiously, almost afraid to hear the answer."

"I mean things like blackmail or nasty rumors that ruined their reputations or families. There were even a few people whose businesses went down the toilet and they ended up having to declare bankruptcy. Now everyone's too scared to even try. Given their positions of power, the whole family basically has local law enforcement in their pocket. Nothing happens around here without their say-so."

My lip curled up. "God, these people sound terrible."

She nodded resolutely. "They really are. The best thing you could do is stay off their radar all together."

"Consider me warned. I'll steer clear," I reassured, trying to put her mind at ease.

She stuffed half of a donut into her mouth like she needed the spike of sugar to keep going before diving back in.

"About fifteen years ago, there was a local girl named Layne Denning who went missing. She'd been dating Tolliver Brady all through high school, but the two of them had broken up shortly before she disappeared. It was never confirmed, but the rumor was that she'd dumped him for the son of one of the Wraiths. As you can imagine, Tolliver wasn't the kind of guy to take that news very well. No one knows the full story, but it's said he started stalking and harassing her. Making threats to try and scare her into taking him back. Then one day she was just gone." She snapped her fingers dramatically. "Just like that. No one would say it out loud, but most people were convinced Tolliver had something to do with it, but the Bradys banded together and pointed the finger at the Iron Wraiths. Accused the kid of doing something to her and claimed the club helped to cover it up.

I hadn't realized until that moment that I'd been holding my breath, enraptured by her story. "Did anyone ever find out what happened to Layne?"

She shook her head, her eyes filling with sadness. "No. The Sheriff's Department in Redemption, the next town over, even got involved, helping with the search but there was no sign of her. Nothing ever turned up. It was like she disappeared in a puff of smoke."

I pressed my hand to my chest against my pounding heart. "God, that's so sad."

Iris sniffled. "I know. I knew Layne. She was a couple years older than me. She was such a sweet girl. The Iron Wraiths didn't take too kindly to their reputation being smeared, so after that, they went out of their way to step in where the Bradys were concerned and pushed back. From there, it just kind of grew. Now it's sort of this unspoken rule around here that if you need help and can't trust the police, you can go to the Wraiths and they'll take care of it for you. Like, there was a waitress from the diner a few years back who's boyfriend beat her so bad he put her in the hospital. The police didn't do anything because the loser was a drinking buddy of the former Chief's, so of course they took his side."

"Let me guess. The former Chief was a Brady?"

She nodded solemnly. "Tolliver's father, Randy. And

if that wasn't bad enough, when Randy retired a few years back, his son stepped right into the position."

Geez. This was the kind of thing you'd expect to watch on a daytime soap, not see in real life. "What happened after that?"

She leaned in, lowering her voice like there was anyone around that could overhear. "The boyfriend was found unconscious in an alley, beaten to within an inch of his life. I mean, the guy was a *mess*, barely recognizable. They had to keep him in a medically induced coma while they tried to get the swelling on his brain to go down. Once he came out of it, he was basically in a full body cast, even had to have his shattered jaw wired shut."

I rocked back in shock. "And it was the motorcycle club that did it?"

An infinitesimal smile tugged at her lips as she shrugged. "That's the thing, no one can prove that it was them. They're wily like that, not a single piece of evidence linking them to anything, and the boyfriend was so freaking scared, he refused to say a word about what happened. Just kept claiming he fell down some stairs after a night of drinking. But the Brady's suspected and wouldn't let it go until a handful of them were arrested. But with no proof and the victim keeping his busted mouth shut and refusing to press charges, they couldn't hold them for long. Not long after they got out, the boyfriend decided to move away, out of the blue."

My heart was beating faster thanks to the story she just told me. I had no idea the history of this town was so . . . dark, and I would have been lying if I said I wasn't concerned. I could only hope I was able to stay far away from all the drama. I was just looking for an easy life. Getting mixed up in what she'd just told me was the very last thing I wanted to do.

My cheeks puffed out, my lips pursing as I blew out a long gust of air. "Wow. That's . . . a lot."

"I know I just laid a lot on you, but honestly, aside from a few bad apples, this really is a great town. I don't want you to think you made a mistake moving here."

I looked around at my new home. While it was in desperate need of furniture, just being inside of it made me happy, and I still had that feeling deep in my gut telling me I'd made the right choice in settling here. Like she said, it was only a few bad apples, and I was determined not to let them ruin my fresh start.

"I don't regret it," I finally announced, giggling when Iris's shoulders sagged in relief.

"I'm so glad to hear that. And I mean that as your new friend, not your realtor." She hopped off the counter and slapped my knee. "Now let's get moving."

My body moved of its own accord, sliding off the counter, clutching my coffee tightly with one hand and snatching up one last donut with the other as I followed her out of the kitchen. "What? Where are we going?"

"Furniture shopping. A human being can't possibly live like this. And on the way, you're going to tell me how Courtland Pope is in bed." She looked back over her shoulder and waggled her brows. "Spare no detail. Because I've seen the guy, and I can only imagine."

SEVEN

THE GARAGE WAS in full swing by the time I turned the handles of my bike and guided it past the open gate of the chain-link fence that surrounded the property and rolled up to the spot right outside the office. Each bay already had a car in it currently being worked on, as well as a line three deep outside the rolled up doors. Business was good, and usually that was enough to put me in a good mood, especially on a day when the sun was high and bright in a clear blue sky. Perfect weather for a long ride.

In a matter of months, the weather would start to change, and my bike would have to be put away for the winter, so this was typically my favorite time of year. But there wasn't much that could improve the shit mood I'd been in the past two days—ever since I woke up hard as a rock and ready to sink my cock back into a certain raven-haired beauty, only to find she'd snuck out some time while I slept—even a brilliant sunny day wasn't enough.

I killed the engine and shoved the kickstand down with the heel of my boot, throwing my leg over to stand just as the door to the Iron Wraith's clubhouse across the courtyard swung open and Bane stepped out, blinking red-rimmed eyes against the sunlight as he scratched at his stomach with one hand and lifted a beer to his lips with the other. It was barely eight in the morning, but odds were, he and some of the other younger members had been at it all night and were only just starting to wind down. Or still going—who the hell knew with them.

When I'd been that age, I basically lived at the club house just like they did, taking a woman to the room I kept in the back to fuck before sending her on her way, or crashing after a night of too much partying. I spent more time there than anywhere else, choosing to surround myself with the family I'd chosen for myself as frequently as possible. But once I stepped into the role of president, I'd quickly come to to realize that privacy was a gift. The headaches that came with my new position in the club made having my own space necessary for the sake of my sanity. I needed somewhere I could kick back and decompress in peace and quiet.

I loved my club, don't get me wrong. I loved everything about being a Wraith and the brotherhood that came with it, but with the president patch came a fuck ton of responsibility, at least that had been the case since I stepped in and started turning my club in a different direction than the one it had been on since its inception.

My old man had been president before me and had been content to ride the wave of the men in power that had come before him. Back then, the Iron Wraiths had their hand in all sorts of shit, making money by moving guns and offering protection to some seriously nasty fucking people who ran drugs up from the border. If it was lucrative, no matter how illegal, we had our hand in that pot. The only thing we didn't dabble in was the trafficking of people.

I'd joined up as soon as I was old enough, prospecting in because I didn't know any other life. The Wraiths were in my blood and had been for generations. It was just assumed I'd step up to be a part of my old man's legacy when the time came. But once I had my cut and was brought into the fold completely, seeing the shit my brothers were doing for cash, well, it left a sour taste in my mouth. It was bad enough those fucking Bradys were destroying my town from the inside out, the people that were supposed to serve and protect sitting cozy in their fucking pockets. With us on the wrong side of things, that meant there was no one looking out for the people in Ashland. My people. I'd grown up here, born and raised, and I'd witnessed the suffering. I couldn't just sit back and watch it keep happening.

The transition away from all that shit hadn't been easy. We'd lost a number of guys back then, men who chose to walk away from their brothers because they wanted things to stay how they'd been for decades. They liked the money too much to give a damn about going legit. That had been a dark time for the club, and there were times I worried I was making a mistake or that the Iron Wraiths wouldn't make it through the changes I was trying to implement. It had been a struggle—hell, it was downright painful—but I'd eventually steered us through, and we were now stronger than ever.

Bane's head twisted in my direction, his beer hand coming up. "Mornin' Prez."

I jerked my head in acknowledgement. "Don't you have shit you're supposed to be doin' right now?" I called back.

I could see the whites of his teeth sparkling all the way from where I stood as he grinned. The man came by his nickname honestly, at least. He could be the bane of my fucking existence when he wanted to be, which was more often than not. "Figured I'd shower the Jameson off before headin' into work. Be there in ten."

I let out a grunt he couldn't hear before turning on my boot and climbing the metal stairs to the office door. The A/C unit in the window was blasting cool air out into the small room to combat the stuffiness that came from having two large windows that allowed the sunlight to pour in, making the whole place feel like a goddamn greenhouse.

Pops sat behind the desk, a pair of wire-framed glasses perched on his nose as he leaned in close to the computer screen, his eyes narrowed into slits as his index fingers hunted and pecked along the keyboard. The cut he wore was so old and worn in that the black leather had faded to gray, but he still wore those patches with pride every damn day. Pops was one of the founding members of the Iron Wraiths and after my father had passed, had become the one person who's council I always sought out when I felt like I was being set adrift. I wasn't sure I'd have made it through my club's transition if it hadn't been for his guidance.

"Those things on your face are supposed to help you see better, old man. They're not doin' their job if you gotta be up on the screen like that."

Pops took off the cheaters and tossed them onto the desk that was currently covered with papers, so many you couldn't even see the top of the damn thing. "You keep givin' me shit and I'll let you handle your own invoicing. How's that sound?"

A huff of laughter passed my lips as I moved to the ancient coffee machine on top of the shelf beneath the foggy glass that looked out over the garage. The thing was a piece of shit that brewed coffee nearly the consistency of tar, but buying a replacement always managed to slip my mind until the time came when I had to pour myself a cup. I'd tell myself I'd remember to run out and get a new one every time, but it never failed that something else would pop up to take my mind in a different direction, and the cycle would just continue.

I lifted the paper cup and drank, my lips curling back from my teeth on a wince at that first taste.

I let the caffeine do its work as I looked out at the bustling garage. It never failed to give me a hit of pride when I saw how well the place was doing. There had been a lot of concern years back that we wouldn't be able to make the same kind of money going legit, but I'd busted my ass to build up the garage and a few other businesses the club owned so my men wouldn't feel the sting for long. On top of regular maintenance such as oil changes, tire rotations, and inspections that kept us flush, we were booked two years out on custom built bikes. It was those projects that really had the money rolling in.

The one thing I'd held on to despite it's less than legal status was the underground fighting ring the club had started back in the day, mainly because it was a favorite way for a lot of my guys to blow off steam. The club took a decent cut of every fight, but the biggest paydays came when it was a Wraith in the ring. It just so happened my guys were really fucking good at fighting, so when a

Wraith was on the ticket, it never failed that the club would rake it in.

"Thought this was supposed to be your day off," Pops grunted as he pushed out of his chair and came over to join me, pouring himself what was probably his third cup already. He didn't seem bothered by the shit. Not that I was surprised. The man had an iron stomach. Had to if the years of hard living he'd put in hadn't taken their toll on the man yet. "Don't you have anything better to do than hang around here?"

I tossed back the rest of my coffee and crumpled the cup, tossing it into the trashcan beside the door. "I'm not on the clock. Just here to spend some time workin' on the Cougar is all."

My own passion project sat at the very back of the garage beneath a cover, just waiting for me to get my hands on her. The '67 Mercury Cougar GT was going to be a thing of fucking beauty once I finally finished her, but finding the time to work on restoring her was easier said than done. "Been too long since I was under her hood."

Pops let out a thoughtful hum. "Is it really the Cougar's hood you're thinkin' of getting under?"

I lifted my brows. "What are you goin' on about? It's not time to put your ass in an old folk's home, is it?"

"I'm just askin' if you're here, blowin' off steam,

'cause you're still butt hurt over a certain pretty girl taking off like a thief in the night."

My head whipped in his direction, my eyes narrowing. "Fuck off, old man. See if I tell you shit anymore."

He let out a burst of laughter, clapping me on the shoulder before turning and heading back to the desk as I moved out into the garage, heading straight for the Cougar. If it wasn't for him, the state of the paperwork for the garage would be in dire straits, that was for damn sure. There wasn't much on this green earth I hated more than paperwork. But in that moment, I would have loved nothing more than to knock him on his ass.

Mainly because the bastard was right.

As much as I didn't want to admit it, I *was* still butt hurt over a pretty girl. A knockout to be exact. Christ, my dick got hard every time I thought back to my night with Lennon. That woman had looked like something out of a fairytale, all that smooth, porcelain skin, midnight hair, and those pale green-gray eyes that reminded me of sea foam. She looked like a real life Snow White, a fairytale princess I wanted to defile. Then I got my hands on her and she went absolutely fucking wild. The way she writhed on that car as I fucked her with my fingers was nearly enough to have me blowing in my jeans, something I hadn't done since I was a kid, for fuck's sake. But once I got her home? Jesus, the things we'd done, the way she begged for more, even when I worried I was being too rough. She'd been insatiable. I couldn't remember the last time I'd met a woman who could keep up with my appetite, but she met my need every step of the goddamn way.

I'd known the moment I first laid eyes on her that she was who I wanted to spend my night with. What I hadn't expected was for her to get under my skin as thoroughly as she had. I had never taken a woman back to my place for a fuck. I either went home with them, took them back to the clubhouse if they were into that, or fucked them in a dark corner of whatever bar we were in. And I *never* put them on the back of my bike. That shit just wasn't done.

But Lennon had cast some sort of spell on me as I sat inside Toni's talking and laughing with her over tequila shots and beer. By the time I asked her to leave with me, there was this living, breathing thing clawing at the inside of my chest, desperate to get out and mark the woman as mine. I wanted her so bad there was no chance of waiting. I needed to see her come apart under my hands, and it was so goddamn hot, I'd nearly lost my mind. The only thought in my head after making her come on my fingers, after that first little taste of her, was to get her ass on the back of my bike and take her home with me so I could spend the rest of the night buried as deep inside her pussy as I could possibly get.

And mark her I had. Her tits were covered in hickeys

by the time I finally passed out. But I wasn't the only one who'd turned into an animal. When I'd gotten in the shower later that morning, I'd found her scratch marks across my back and shoulders along with tiny bruises in the shape of her teeth on my pecs and abs. We'd spent the entire night ravaging each other, and I wasn't nearly done. I'd wanted to wake up and start all over again. But when I reached across the sheets, they'd been cold and empty.

One night was usually the extent of what I had to give a woman, but I wanted more of Lennon, so it was a real kick in the balls to wake up and find she'd bounced before I had my fill. It had been two days and I could still taste her pussy on my tongue and feel it wrapped around my cock. That craving had only gotten worse. I wanted more, damn it, and I didn't have the first clue how to find her.

I spent the morning and afternoon taking my frustrations out on the Cougar, ripping out the molded, tattered interior and stripping off the quarter paneling that had been rusted completely through. Most people would have taken one look at that car and sent it straight to the junk yard. More of it was trash than not. But I saw what it could be—what it *would* be, at least once I was finished with her. And she was going to be a thing of beauty.

It had been a long time since I had a chance to rebuild a car from the ground up, but once I got in there, it was just like riding a bike. It all came back to me, and as I worked in silence, the hours ticking down, I felt myself start to relax and my mind clear.

At least until my phone rang in my back pocket.

I wiped my hand on a rag and pulled it out, seeing my niece's name flashing across the screen.

"Hey, sweetheart. How's it going?"

"Uncle Court?" The quiver in her voice instantly put me on edge, and I knew whatever reason she had for calling me was going to piss me right the hell off. "Can you come get me? Mom forgot me at school again."

God. Fucking. Damn it.

EIGHT

LENNON

IF THE FIRST day at my new job had taught me anything, it was that things had changed far beyond what I could have possibly imagined since the last time I'd set foot in a classroom. Kids now a days spoke a completely different language than they had back when I'd first started teaching.

And I meant that literally.

They used words that I recognized, but in ways that made no sense to me at all. Apparently "cap" had a totally different meaning now, but "no cap" meant something else entirely. And boys now a days strove for something called rizz, which I was still pretty confused about, but was piecing together meant something along the lines of swagger? Or at least I hoped. It was hard to follow along with the conversations. And don't even get me started on whatever the hell *skibbity* was supposed to mean.

I'd lost count of how many times I had to tell a student I wasn't their bro or *bruh* and to please refer to me as Ms. Cody. I'd always felt young for thirty-five, convinced that there was still so much life ahead of me, but by the time the bell rang to dismiss my last class of the day, I couldn't remember ever feeling so old in my life. For the love of God, to hear these kids tell it, I was practically geriatric. And if I had one more student ask me what it was like before Netflix or how things were "in my time" my head was going to explode.

When in the ever loving hell had thirty-five become middle age?

The second the last student walked out of my classroom, I collapsed into the chair behind my desk and dropped my head into my hands with a pained groan, wishing I had booze on hand. My head was pounding harder than it had from my hangover the week prior. I would have been lying if I said I wasn't questioning whether or not I was still cut out for this. I just hadn't expected so much to change in the years I'd been working for Oliver's family. I felt like I was starting at square one, and I was already at a serious disadvantage.

"Tough first day?"

I lifted my head, forcing a smile to curl my lips as I took in the woman standing in my classroom doorway.

She was a tall, willowy blonde in a pencil skirt and high heels that I immediately coveted. "Oh no. It was great," I lied, trying by best to keep a brave face. "They were great. Everything was great. I'm just tired. Didn't get much sleep last night."

That part of it was the truth, at least. I'd been so anxious for my first day I'd spent the night tossing and turning. You would have thought I was one of the kids, nervous about making friends and fitting in, not a freaking adult.

The woman scoffed, pushing off the doorframe and moving into the room. "I might have believed you if you hadn't said great too many times," she stated as she folded herself into one of the front row desks right across from me. "We teach middle school, love. Most days are raging dumpster fires. And those are the good ones."

I blinked, taking her in before my head fell back on a deep, rolling belly laugh. By the time I collected myself I had tears streaking down my cheeks. "Okay. You may have a point."

"Of course I do." She smiled, pushing her thick panel of flaxen hair over her shoulder. "The kids call me Ms. Fletcher, but you can call me Phoebe. I teach seventh grade science. Welcome to Ashland Middle School."

"Thanks. I'm Lennon Cody."

"Nice to meet you, Lennon. Now how about you tell me how your first day really was?"

I let out a sigh, my entire body slumping in defeat. "It was exhausting," I confessed, feeling weary down to my bones. "I knew this would be difficult, coming back after such a long break, but I honestly don't know how I'm going to be able to keep up."

She waved her hand. "You're going to be fine, trust me. You just have to get your feet wet again. Just have a little faith in yourself, and remember, you can't let them see you're scared. It's like throwing chum in the water when there are great whites swimming all around."

"Noted," I said, humor lightening my voice. "And thanks for the encouragement. I really needed it."

She unfolded herself from the desk, her movements loose and graceful. "We'll do lunch tomorrow in the teacher's lounge. I'll give you the lay of the land."

I smiled my first genuine smile of the day. "You're on. Thanks."

"Any time, love. We have to stick together or they'll win."

With one last wave, Phoebe headed out of my classroom, leaving me feeling so much better about my likelihood of surviving this job.

I was in the middle of working on my lesson plan for the following week, wanting to get ahead so I'd at least have a leg up on the hellions I called students, when my cellphone started to ring from inside my purse.

I fished around inside, trying to find it, and eventually located it at the very bottom beneath my wallet, a few stray tampons, the tiny notepad I kept for grocery lists, and a three-month-old receipt from a fast food place.

I swiped to answer, not recognizing the number that had popped up on the screen.

"Hello?"

"Lennon?"

My back shot straight, my voice coming out in a squeak. "Oliver?"

My ex-husband's panicked voice shot through the phone. "Oh, thank god. I've been going out of my mind! I've been trying to reach you for days. Are you all right? Christ, Lennon, where have you been?" he asked, finishing off his tirade in an accusatory tone.

I pulled the phone away from my ear and looked at it like it might grow fangs and strike at any moment. I'd blocked all of Oliver's numbers, his work, his cell, even the outdated land line he'd still insisted on having for *emergencies*.

"What number are you calling me from?" I finally asked after returning the phone to my ear.

There was a brief pause before he spoke. "I borrowed Jason's phone," he confessed before the rest of his words rushed out. "But only because you were dodging my calls and I didn't know how else to get through to you."

Red coated my vision, heat building in my cheeks as

my blood began to boil. "I can't believe you used one of your friends' phones to call me! I'm not dodging your calls, Oliver. I blocked you," I gritted out, my molars grinding together as I tried my hardest not to explode. The school day might have been over, but there were still kids and teachers milling around. The last thing I wanted to do was cause a scene on my first day. "You and I have nothing left to talk about. We're done. You need to get that through your head." I reached up, dragging my fingers through my hair in frustration. "I can't even begin to explain how inappropriate it is that you used someone else's phone to trick me into answering."

"You left me no other choice," he barked through the line. "You cut me off. I had no other way of reaching you."

"Because we're divorced!" I started to shout before catching myself and lowering my voice. "I didn't cut you off, Oliver. I divorced you," I hissed in a hushed voice. "That means there's no longer any reason for you to ever need to reach me. We're done. There's nothing left for us to talk about."

"Don't be like that, baby."

Baby. My top lip curled up at the unimaginative endearment. He *still* couldn't bring himself to put any effort into things like that.

"I'm not your baby. Not anymore. You need to stop calling me." I hung up before he could get another word out, immediately scrolling through to block that number as well. If I had to change my own damn number for him to take the hint, that was what I'd do, but that was a last resort.

With a heavy sigh, I packed my stuff up in the brown leather messenger tote I'd gotten the day Iris and I went furniture shopping. We'd hit up a few stores, getting a couple pieces like a bed and a loveseat, but buying all new furniture was proving to be more difficult than I thought it would be. My old house was decorated the way Oliver liked, the furniture picked out by his mother, and I'd hated every single bit of it. At the time, I'd convinced myself that I didn't mind. What did it matter that the sofa was a bit stuffy for my taste and not all that comfortable to sit on, making relaxing impossible? Those things didn't matter compared to a loving, happy marriage.

God, I'd been such an idiot.

I'd lived so many parts of my life for that man that I hadn't even realized just how much of myself I'd lost until I stood in the middle of a furniture store, trying to decide which way my tastes leaned. Iris had been there to tell me it was okay, that there was still plenty of time to figure it all out, and instead of letting me get down about it, she'd insisted we go shopping to get me a whole new wardrobe for my new job. A job that *I* chose.

A job I was determined to do great at, despite my less than stellar first day.

The halls were quiet as I headed out. The only person aside from me was the janitor mopping the floors that had been tramped on by what felt like a million kids all day long. I returned his friendly smile and gave him a wave as I headed for the exit, only to pull up short the moment I stepped through the heavy glass doors.

I recognized the pretty blonde girl sitting on one of the concrete benches outside the school. She'd been in one of my earlier classes, but I couldn't recall her name. Her head was down, her long hair obscuring her face, but as I got closer, I was able to hear her sniffle and see her lift her hand to brush at her cheeks.

"Hi." Her head shot up at the sound of my voice, her striking dark brown eyes watery and rimmed with red like she'd been crying. I lifted my hands in surrender, not wanting to frighten her as I got drew closer. "Sorry, I didn't mean to scare you."

She batted at her damp cheeks with the back of her hand as she gave me a wobbly smile that didn't come close to meeting her eyes. "It's okay."

There was a voice in the back of my head telling me I needed to stay with this girl, so instead of heading to the car, I pointed at the empty stretch of bench beside her. "Mind if I sit?"

"No." She shook her head quickly. "I mean sure.

Yeah." She scooched over another few inches to give me more room. "I mean, no, I don't mind if you sit. Have a seat. If you want."

Unhooking my bag from my shoulder, I propped it against the leg of the bench and took a seat, letting the stress of the day go with a long, heavy sigh before finally addressing her. "You look like you're having about as good a day as I am."

Her head canted to the side in curiosity. "You had a bad day?"

"Well, not bad. That's the wrong word, I suppose. Taxing would be more appropriate." I looked at her and smiled. "And exhausting. I've been out of the game for a while, and teaching is *not* like riding a bike," I joked. "It isn't really something you just remember how to do."

The girl's shoulders sagged on a deep exhale as she tucked her hair behind her ear. "I think you did pretty good. Especially for your first day."

She couldn't have possible known how much it meant for me to hear that. It was one thing to be reassured by another teacher, but for a student to tell me I didn't completely suck was a serious relief. "Thanks. I really appreciate that."

We sat silently for a few seconds as I tried to figure out how to play this. I didn't just want to jump out and ask if she was all right and risk having her shut down.

Fortunately, she decided to pick the conversation back up on her own before I had to. "It's Ms. Cody, right?"

"That's me. You're in my second period class."

"Yeah. Marigold." She placed her hand on her chest, reminding me of her name.

"Marigold," I repeated quietly, a soft smile curling my lips upward. "Such a pretty name. Do people call you Mari?"

Her cheeks and the tips of her ears flushed red as she ducked her head down, a bashful yet genuine smile pulling at her lips. "No. They mainly just call me Marigold. Except for my uncle." Her smile grew brighter at the mention of him. "He calls me Goldie."

Goldie, I thought, my own grin tugging wide. That was incredibly sweet, and I could tell by the way her sadness momentarily disappeared and a glow formed in her eyes as she spoke of her uncle that he was special to her.

I bumped my shoulder against hers. "You know what? I think that nickname fits you."

She sniffled again, rubbing the back of her hand under her nose. "Thanks," she said quietly.

I took a moment to think over how to say what I wanted to say without spooking the girl next to me, relying solely on my gut instinct—something that had been lying dormant for years as I kidded myself into thinking I was happy as a receptionist when it wasn't my calling. I could have been playing this all wrong, but I had to at least try. "I won't push you to tell me why you're upset if you don't want to talk about it. That's yours to keep if you choose, but I am going to ask you if you're okay. And it would be really great if you were honest with me."

She blinked, her large, deep brown eyes full of emotion. I expected her to say she was fine and to leave it at that, but she surprised me when she opened her mouth and the words spilled out. "My mom forgot to pick me up." Her voice was quiet and riddled with sadness.

My brows dipped low in the middle. "Oh, Marigold. I'm so sorry. I'm sure she's just running late. I bet she'll be here any minute, but I'm happy to wait with you."

She shook her head, looking back down at her feet as she wrapped her arms around her middle like she was trying to protect herself. "No, she's not coming. It's not the first time she's forgotten me."

That tugged painfully at my heart because I knew how badly it hurt to feel unimportant or unwanted. My mother had passed away when I was really little and after that, my father had pretty much shut down. It was like he didn't know how to exist without her in his life. And he knew even less how to be the father of a little girl who was struggling without a female presence to help guide her. Growing up, he hadn't ever had much time for me, and I couldn't help but feel like he didn't really want me around, like I was a painful reminder of a past he would have rather forgotten about.

When I left home for college it was as though he'd been relieved that I wouldn't be there anymore. There were no calls asking if I'd be coming back for holidays or summer breaks. Hell, there were hardly any phone calls at all. My bedroom wasn't waiting untouched for me whenever I came for a visit. In fact, he had barely waited a week before tossing out everything I didn't take with me and turning it into a home gym. I took that as his silent way of communicating that it was no longer my home, not that it had ever felt like much of one.

I didn't need a therapist to tell me that was why I failed to see the entire field of red flags in my marriage. I just wanted so badly for someone to want me back that when Oliver showed interest, I'd glommed on. As the years passed, I ignored all the bad because I didn't want to lose the first true connection I'd ever had to another person.

As I sat on that hard stone bench, I could see those pieces of me in the girl at my side, and it made my chest to tighten painfully.

"I'm happy to give you a ride home, Marigold. Or maybe there's someone else I can call for you?"

She shook her head, pulling her bottom lip between

her teeth. "No thanks. I already called my uncle. He should be here any minute."

Just then, the rumble of a loud engine cut through the air as a large black Ram truck came flying down the road. Her face instantly brightened as it whipped into the parking lot heading right toward us. "There he is. That's my Uncle Court."

My head jerked back around so fast my hair smacked me in the face, my eyes bugging out. "Uncle Court?" That couldn't have possibly been a coincidence. Could it? I mean, how many people in this small town could have that same name?

"Yeah." She smiled happily. "His name's actually Courtland, but I'm the only one allowed to call him Court," she said, preening proudly.

Nope. Definitely *not a coincidence.*

My focus moved back to the truck just as it came to a stop, and the man who I hadn't been able to stop thinking about since our night together threw the door open and climbed out.

A man I'd been counting on never seeing again.

Freaking small towns!

NINE

POPE

I HAD the accelerator pressed all the way to the floorboard the entire way to my niece's middle school, cutting the twenty-minute drive nearly in half thanks to the anger that was pushing me faster the entire way. By the time I jerked the wheel of my truck, guiding it into the parking lot of the school that was now empty—considering the place had been closed down for more than an hour—I was fuming, barely able to keep my rage in check as I silently cursed my sister, Angela.

She had always been a little flighty, even as a kid, and it sure as hell didn't help that our father had spoiled the damn woman rotten. But it had only gotten worse as she got older. She was his little princess who could do no wrong, and instead of eventually growing the fuck up, she'd clung to that title he'd given her and basically let him continue to do everything for her.

When he died six years ago it had hit everyone hard, but Angela had shattered. Rather than pulling her shit together for her daughter, she spiraled, and without our old man to take care of her, she'd started latching on to every loser and piece of shit out there who'd give her the time of day. She put all those dickheads over her own kid, basically leaving my sweet, innocent Marigold to take care of herself while she went looking for her next relationship every time a shithead boyfriend dumped her ass because they couldn't deal with a clingy, emotionally manipulative basket case who expected to be catered to.

Her self-centered attitude and borderline narcissism had been pissing me off for years now, but when it started effecting my niece, well, that was just something I couldn't abide. The moment that girl had been born, she'd become my favorite person on the face of the planet, my reason for being, and the thought that my sister was neglecting her set my blood on fire, the heat traveling through my veins burning so goddamn hot it was a wonder smoke wasn't pouring from my ears.

"Uncle Court!" my Goldie called out the moment I swung out of my truck. Her smile lit up her face and warmed my heart as she ran toward me, the backpack hanging from her shoulders bouncing with each step.

At thirteen, she was already taller than half the kids in her grade, just like I'd been, and her features favored mine more than her mother's. In fact, she looked so much like me, she could have been my kid, and it wasn't unusual for people to confuse her for my daughter. Where Angela took after our mom with darker hair and brown eyes several shades lighter than my own, Marigold and I had both taken after my old man with blonde hair and nearly black eyes.

She was the only person in existence who could get away with calling me Court. That name was for her and her alone.

"Hey, honey," I greeted, reaching out just as soon as she was close enough and yanking her against me in a hug that most likely bordered on too tight. But I couldn't help myself. When she'd called to say her mom had forgotten her at school, a million different scenarios had run through my head, each one worse than the last.

It wasn't until I pulled into the school's parking lot and saw all that sunny hair that I was able to take a full breath, knowing she was all right. I didn't know what the hell I'd do if anything ever happened to her. She was my light. Thinking of harm coming to her caused me physical pain.

I pulled back and took her cheeks in my hands, tipping her face back to get a good look at her. The whites of her eyes were red and glassy, letting me know my girl had been crying. "You good?"

She sniffled, nodding her head in the affirmative. Her

smile wobbled a little bit, but it still managed to reach her eyes, which worked wonders in loosening the knots that had been tangled up in my chest since I got her phone call.

"I'm good, Unka," she said, using the nickname she'd given me when she was barely a toddler and couldn't say the word *uncle* correctly. "My new teacher actually stayed with me." She turned and pointed back in the direction she'd just come running from.

I'd been so consumed with worrying about Marigold, that I hadn't realized there was someone with her until that moment. Lifting my head, my gaze connected with a pair of familiar green-gray eyes. I didn't have to get any closer to know those very eyes were flecked with gold and brown and had a ring of gunmetal gray around the iris. I'd seen them up close and personal when I'd been buried deep inside her during our night together. I'd had so much time to study those eyes that night that I'd know them anywhere. I knew how they looked when she was excited, when she was turned on, when I was about to get her off, and my favorite, when she came down after I'd made her come. The way her eyes would get all droopy and hazy as a tiny little smile tugged at her lips made me hard for her all over again.

There was no smile on her full, pouty pink lips just then. She looked like a deer caught in the headlights as she slowly rose from the bench she'd been sitting on lifting her hand in a hesitant wave. All that long, flowing black hair hung down her back in waves that shined beneath the sunlight.

"Raven?"

A deep blush stained her cheeks at the nickname I'd given her that night.

Marigold's brows knitted together in confusion. "No, that's Ms. Cody." She latched onto my hand, her own so much smaller and more delicate as she tugged me in Lennon's direction. "Ms. Cody, this is my Uncle Court, but everyone else calls him Pope. Unka, this is my new English teacher, Ms. Cody." My niece turned to look back at the woman who'd been plaguing every fucking one of my thoughts for days. She smiled at Lennon like the woman walked on water. "She waited with me for you to get here."

I gave myself a few seconds to give her a once over in appreciation, scanning her incredible body from the toes of her chunky-heeled ankle boots to the top of her head. If I thought she could wear the fuck out of a pair of jeans like the night I first met her, then the short sleeved black dress with white polka-dots she was currently wearing was even better. There was nothing that was meant to be sexy about it. It came down to mid-calf, for Christ's sake. But it was like the line of buttons that ran all the way from chest to knees was begging to be undone one by one. Preferably with my teeth.

Fucking hell. The last thing I needed was to get hard right here in front of a middle school with my niece standing two feet away.

"Thank you for lookin' out for my girl."

That flush on Lennon's face creeped down her neck to her chest. She tried to hide it, but I caught the slight tremble in her hand as she lifted it to tuck a lock of hair behind her ear, and it took everything in me not to grin, knowing she was still as effected by our night together as I was.

"It's no big deal. I enjoyed hanging out with her. She's a great kid."

Marigold practically preened under her new teacher's praise, causing something in my chest to tighten. Lennon could have said she was just doing her job or something along those lines, but instead, she made my girl feel special.

I pulled my niece into my side and bent to press a kiss to the crown of her head. "Do me a favor, sweetheart, and wait in the truck for me, yeah? Just want to have a quick word with Ms. Cody here. It'll only take a minute."

She bounced on her toes and gripped onto the straps of her backpack. "Okay. Bye, Ms. Cody."

Lennon smiled and lifted her hand in a wave. "Bye, Marigold. See you tomorrow."

I kept my head turned, my gaze on my girl until she

was safely tucked into the passenger seat of my truck before looking back at Lennon.

Without Goldie as a buffer, I could see the nerves in the way she tangled her fingers in front of her and fidgeted from foot to foot. "Um." She rolled her lips between her teeth and bit down. "Hi."

A smirk pulled at my mouth, curling my lips upward as my gaze ran down the curve of her neck, taking in all that pretty pink flesh stretched across her collarbones and dipping down below the V of her neckline. "I'd say this was a hell of a lucky coincidence," I rasped, my tone low and dripping with the desire I felt as all the blood in my body traveled south. I took a step closer, needing to be near her. "Haven't been able to get you off my mind since you snuck out on me."

Her throat worked on a swallow as her sea foam eyes bounced all over the place, looking anywhere but at me. "Uh, yeah. That was a fun night."

My brows winged up toward my hairline. "A fun night?" I repeated on a bewildered laugh. "Is that what you'd call it?"

A pucker formed between her brows as she frowned in confusion. "Well . . . yeah. I mean, what would you call it?"

I took another step closer, noticing the way her pulse fluttered wildly along her delicate neck. I lowered my voice even more just in case someone chose that moment to walk out of the school. "I'd call it the best fuckin' sex of my life."

Her eyes flashed with surprise. "Oh . . ."

I couldn't handle being so close to her and not touching her, not when I could still remember exactly how sweet her pussy tasted. Reaching out, I took her chin between my index finger and thumb, using my hold to tip her face up to mine. Those full, pouty lips of hers parted, forming a tiny O as she blinked slowly.

"Yeah, baby. I can still remember exactly how it feels to have that hot pussy of yours clench around my cock every time you came."

Her sweet breath gusted past her lips on an exhale. "Pope—"

"Woke up that mornin' wanting more of you, but you bailed before I was ready to let you go. Still get hard thinkin' about that night. Christ, Raven. My balls have been so goddamn blue I've barely been able to function."

Her gaze darted over my shoulder toward my truck. She blinked slowly, and I could practically see shutters slamming into place. Clearing her throat, she took a step back, severing our connection.

"Look, Pope, I had a really great time with you—"

"I'd say you did, darlin'. You had a *really great time* at least five times."

Her nostrils flared, those pale green eyes growing heated like her brain just flipped back to that night, and,

Christ, but it was getting harder and harder to keep my dick from trying to bust through the zipper of my jeans. "As I was saying, I had a great time. You came along and gave me a night I hadn't realized I needed." She closed her eyes and inhaled deeply through her nose like she was trying to get her thoughts together. Something told me I wasn't going to like what came next. "But I don't think it should happen again."

And I was right.

I'd been around the block more than my fair share of times. I knew when a woman wanted me, and this one *definitely* wanted me, but there was something holding her back.

I couldn't remember the last time a woman had gotten under my skin the way she had. I'd broken every one of my rules the night I met her, and instead of having my fill and moving on once the night was over, my craving for her had only gotten stronger.

Closing the distance between us, I lowered my head until my lips brushed against the shell of her ear. "If you can tell me you don't still think about what it feels to have my cock stretching you open, I'll give you this play."

Her body began to tremble, and as I pulled back to look down at her, there was no missing the way her eyes had glazed over. Her tongue darted out and dragged across her bottom lip, and it took everything I had not to eliminate the last few inches between us and pull that tongue into my mouth.

"Say it, baby. Tell me you don't still want me and I'll walk away."

Her breath hitched as she opened her mouth. "I . . ." But nothing else came out. I had her dead to rights. She couldn't even get the lie past her lips.

The corners of my mouth curled upward with a cocky smirk. "That's what I thought."

Her eyes narrowed, flashing with a hint of temper I'd gotten a taste of during our night together whenever I challenged her by pushing her body past its limit. She'd responded by digging her nails into my ass or back hard enough to cause pain, letting me know she wasn't just going to lay there and let me have my way, that she fully intended on participating.

Fuck, but I loved that temper.

"You can try lying to yourself all you want, but we both know you still want me, darlin'. And I'm nowhere near done with you." I started walking backward, that grin on my face stretching into a full-blown smile as I issued another challenge. "This conversation's not over, Raven. Better prepare yourself now, because this . . ." I waved my finger in the space between us, "is inevitable."

TEN
POPE

WALKING AWAY from Lennon earlier hadn't been easy, but I needed to see to my girl. It was bad enough her own mother didn't bother to put her first, I never wanted my niece to feel like she was second to anything else with me. Besides, now that I had Lennon's full name and occupation, tracking her down again would be a hell of a lot easier.

Instead of taking Marigold straight home, I swung my truck into the parking lot of Al's Diner, navigating into a space right by the door, and threw the gearshift into Park.

My girl looked at me with the biggest, brightest smile, letting out a squeal that damn near rendered me deaf. "Are we getting pie?"

Al's Diner was known for boasting that they had the best pie in the state, and fortunately, they weren't lying.

"What else?" I returned her infectious smile as I killed the engine and threw my door open. "In my opinion, a long day at school calls for pie. What do you think?"

She answered by whipping off her seatbelt and bounding out of the truck, bouncing on her toes as she waited on the sidewalk for me to lock up and join her. I threw my arm around her shoulders with a chuckle as I guided her to the door and pulled it open for her. It was the little things in life, like a warm slice of pie after a long day, that mattered most, that was something my father had taught me and something I'd tried my damnedest to pass on to my niece. So seeing her excitement worked wonders in loosening that tension that had been squeezing my chest in a vice grip thanks to my waste-of-space sister.

She skipped through the door, stopping just inside and taking in a deep breath like she'd done since she was a toddler, giving herself a moment to pull all the delicious smells into her lungs. Al's wasn't just famous for their pie, after all. There wasn't a thing on their menu that wasn't good enough to make your mouth water.

"Afternoon, you two." I tipped my chin at Bea. The woman was almost as much an institution to this town as the diner itself. She'd been waiting tables here for as long as I could remember.

"Afternoon, Bea."

Marigold gave her favorite waitress a tiny wave. "Hey, Bea."

Bea propped one elbow on the bar that stretched across the entire front of the restaurant, barstools drilled into the ground adjacent for more seating, and placed her other hand on her ample waist, shooting Marigold a wink. "Let me guess, chocolate cream for you, sweetheart?"

My niece nodded happily. It was the same thing she ordered every time I brought her to Al's for a slice of pie. Chocolate cream was her all-time favorite.

Bea looked to me after receiving confirmation. "And what about you, handsome?"

Unlike my girl, I liked to switch it up. "Think I'll do key lime this time around."

"You got it. Take a seat and I'll get that right over to you."

"I gotta use the bathroom, Unka. Be right back."

"Okay, sugar bear. I'll grab us our usual table." Marigold ducked out from beneath my arm and started bouncing toward the hallway that led back to the restrooms.

I moved to the booth against the back wall where we sat every time we came here. It was like an unspoken rule that when I walked into Al's with Marigold that the booth was ours.

I pulled my phone out of my pocket as I slid into the

bench, scrolling to the texts I'd sent to Angela since Marigold had called me, basically asking her where the fuck she was and how the hell she could just forget her daughter like that. Of course, she hadn't answered any of them. My fingers flew across the screen a I fired off another text, my anger at my little sister steadily growing.

Me: *Swear to Christ, Ang. You better be lying in a fucking ditch somewhere.*

I was still staring down at my phone, willing a response to come through, when the bell over the door rang and drew my attention.

"Fuckin' hell," I grunted under my breath as two men in police uniforms came walking into the diner. The Wraiths had never been personal fans of police in general, but the cops in Ashland were a special brand of corrupt. The younger of the two was newer to the force. North Hastings had been part of the Ashland Police Department for about two years now, and I still hadn't been able to get a clear read on him. The other asshole, however, was a familiar face. Officer Grant Wilfred was one of the worst of all of them—not that there were many who weren't in the pocket of the Brady family— second only to the chief himself, Toliver Brady.

Wilfred did a quick scan of the diner before locking in on me, a dark, vicious grin tugging at his mouth as he started in my direction.

I moved my hands beneath the table, my fingers curling into fists so tight my blunt nails dug crescent moons into the balls of my palms. It took everything in my power to keep from standing up and driving my fist into that fuckers face. As much as I couldn't stand him—hell, I couldn't stand half that fucking police force—it wouldn't have done me any good to get arrested for breaking the fucker's nose and knocking his teeth down his throat. It was something I wouldn't have hesitated to do in the past, but as much as the Wraiths were a huge part of my life, when Marigold was born, I'd made a promise to myself to shield her from that world as much as possible.

Her being born was a large part of why I wanted to take my club legit. I didn't want to lose my brother's but I wanted to do everything I could to protect my girl's future. There were more than a few skeletons in my club's closet, skeletons that had taken lives, that would have landed most of us in a grave or a cell. When things had been at their worst and we were at war with rival clubs over our protection routes or gun supplies, there had been innocents caught in the crossfire. Loved ones of club members—people who knew nothing about Wraith business and never should have been targeted—were hurt. Or worse.

Each one of us had known what we were getting into the moment we prospected into the club. Losing a brother to the life was like losing a piece of yourself, but at least we'd made the choice to put ourselves at risk. Family members were different.

Personally, I'd been sick and fucking tired of losing people I loved, of watching my brother's lose people they loved. I wasn't willing to do it anymore, so I'd made my moves.

And because of that, I couldn't stand up and shove my fist down the throat of a crooked motherfucker who hid everything he did behind a goddamn badge. No matter how bad I wanted to.

"Well, well. Look what the cat dragged in." He walked over with a swagger that made him look exactly like the fool he was, his thumbs tucked into the tactical belt that was squeezed around his waist so tight his fat, paunchy stomach hung over it. His uniform was at least two sizes too small, but he was one of those assholes who thought so highly of himself he could do no wrong. Hell, he probably thought he looked good, not like the balding, middle-aged bastard who was too fat to see his own dick that he actually was.

"Move the fuck on, Wilfred," I growled, not that I expected him to listen.

And of course he didn't. "Didn't know this place catered to criminals."

My chest rattled on a chuckle, my lips curling back

from my teeth. "If you're in here, clearly they don't have that big a problem with it."

That wiped the smile off his ugly face fast enough. In fact, in the blink of an eye, it turned an unnatural shade of maroon and his breathing grew labored in a way that was probably attributed to by a shitty diet and lack of exercise. Christ, it was a wonder he hadn't keeled over from a heart attack yet. But we could still hope.

"You son of a—" Before he could move a step in my direction, his partner was there, clamping a hand down on his shoulder.

"Come on, man. Our order's ready. We need to get back out there."

The rage filling his eyes only got worse as I grinned up at him, lifting my hand to give him a little finger wave. "Yeah, *officer*. Shouldn't you be out there serving and protecting?" I might not have been able to knock him the fuck out, but that didn't mean I couldn't screw with him. And he just made it so damn easy.

The man let out a growl as he tried to shake off North's grip, but the younger cop refused to budge. Bea stepped in just then, placing herself between the two of us and setting the slices of pie down on the table. "One chocolate cream and a key lime. Enjoy."

"Thanks, Bea."

Her expression was pulled into a serious frown as she gave me a nod before turning to the men in uniform and passing along a tied-off plastic bag of two Styrofoam to-go containers. "Your lunch, gentlemen. If you'll follow me to the front, I'll ring you up." Her tone brooked no argument. That was just Bea. She didn't tolerate issues from the outside coming into the diner, and at that very moment, I was glad for it since Marigold rounded the corner at that very moment, oblivious to the tension that had just been swirling around as she glided past the two cops and headed straight for our table.

"Ooh, yay!" she exclaimed as she slid into the bench across from me and snatched up her fork, her eyes wide as she dove right into her pie. I pushed the bullshit with Wilfred out of my head and focused on my girl, picking up my own fork, digging into my own pie and enjoying this time I had with her.

ELEVEN

POPE

EVERY MUSCLE in my body tensed up the moment I turned on my sister's street and spotted the car sitting in the driveway. It took everything I had not to beat my fist against the wheel and shout out a string of cuss words, because I knew exactly what some random car in her driveway meant. And judging by the way Marigold's shoulders drew up around her ears and her entire demeanor shifted, she did to.

The front door opened just as I pulled my truck up to the curb in front of the house, and a guy wearing a white t-shirt covered in stains that stretched over the beer gut hanging over the waistband of his jeans stepped out, pulling the door closed behind him.

I turned to Marigold, finding her pressed up against the passenger door with her eyes pinned on her lap. "Sweetheart, you know that guy?"

She pulled in a deep breath and nodded. "Yeah," she muttered. "That's Jeff. He's Mom's new boyfriend."

Fuck.

"How long's he been hanging around?"

Her shoulders came up in a shrug before dropping down heavily. "I don't know. Couple weeks, maybe?"

A couple weeks in pre-teen speak could mean anything from two actual weeks to a month, or longer. Spending time with Marigold had taught me that kids her age had no real concept of time. What felt like an eternity to them was barely a blip on most people's radar.

The hair on the back of my neck prickled as I asked the one question I dreaded most. "He hasn't given you any trouble, has he?"

My past was the very definition of sketchy. I knew how to get rid of a body in a way it would never be found. I'd done it before, and if this prick right here had fucked with my niece, I wouldn't lose a single second of sleep over ending him.

She shook her head without hesitation. "No. He mostly just ignores me. But he does . . . other stuff."

My lungs seized up, making it damn near impossible to pull in a full breath. I did my best to keep my tone even and my face blank, but my girl knew me, and she managed to see right through my mask when I asked, "Other stuff like what?"

Her shoulders hunched like she was trying to curl in on herself, her voice going small in a way that made that rage bubble to the surface again. I swear to Christ, it was a wonder I hadn't ripped the steering wheel clean off.

"He-he gives her stuff. Like pills. And I'm pretty sure they aren't for headaches."

I could *not* lose my shit in front of my niece, no matter how badly I wanted to. "You've seen him do this?"

She nodded. "And I saw her hand him a wad of cash for them. Then when I told her we were out of groceries a couple days later, she told me she didn't have any money and I'd just have to wait until the end of the month."

Christ. My father had to have been rolling over in his grave at what Angela had become. She might have been his princess, but there's no was in hell he'd have been okay with the way she was treating his granddaughter. He'd loved that girl nearly as much as I did, and he would have been sick at hearing this.

"Hey," I said gently, reaching over to take her hand and give it a reassuring squeeze. "I'm gonna fix this, sweetheart. You have my word."

That was all it took to put her at ease, and the trust she had in me, the faith so absolute that I'd protect her that she didn't hesitate to show her relief, was a gift a man like me didn't deserve. I couldn't claim to be a good man. There was too much in my past that proved other-wise. But the people I loved had my whole heart, without question. There wasn't anything I wouldn't do for them.

What I was going to do to Jeff for selling my sister drugs and taking food out of my niece's mouth proved I wasn't a good man. Hell, I was a hypocrite given I used to provide protection for assholes just like him. But when it came to protecting my Goldie, I wouldn't blink, and I damn sure wouldn't lose any sleep over it.

"Thanks, Unka."

I gave her hand one last squeeze before letting go and turning off the truck. "Anything for you, Goldie. Now come on. Let's get you inside."

I threw my door opened and stepped out just as the asshole put his car into gear and started backing out. I took a few seconds to stand on the curb, keeping my gaze locked on him as he reversed out into the street, finally catching sight of me. I made sure to stand where he could see me, and most specifically, the cut I wore over my plain black t-shirt.

Sure enough, he didn't miss it, and I let a menacing smile pull across my face as I watched the color drain from his cheeks. He knew exactly who I was.

Good.

I waited until he passed, taking a good deal of plea-sure in the way his foot slammed down on the accelerator as soon as he passed my truck, squealing his tires in an effort to get away from me. Hell, I wouldn't be surprised if he was texting my sister that very second, breaking up with her ass. Not that it would do him any damn good. It was too late for him. My guy Bane might have been a pain in my ass, but there wasn't anyone he couldn't find. I'd put him on hunting down this asshole, then I'd set him on getting me an address for one Lennon Cody.

But that would have to wait. There was something else I needed to take care of first.

Looping my arm over Marigold's shoulders, I pulled her against my side, being the rock for her to lean on as she gave me her weight, another act of trust that made my chest ache. The front yard had been so neglected the grass was completely fried, crunching beneath the thick rubber soles of my boots. The only green came from the weeds that had choked out all the flowers in the beds and were poking up in the cracks of the walkway.

I twisted the knob and shoved the door open into a dark, gloomy room.

"Jesus Christ," I grunted as I moved to the front window and yanked on the cord of the blinds to let some light in. "It's like a goddamn tomb in here, Angie."

My sister sat in the middle of the couch, kicked back like she didn't have a care in the world. There were empty beer cans littering the coffee table around where she had her feet propped, and she was still dressed in a nightgown and robe even though it was closing in on dinner time. Not that there was any sign of dinner being prepared, and the sink looked like it was filled with every dish they had, all of them dirty. Her hair was a tangled mess, her makeup mussed and smudged. It didn't take a genius to realize what she'd been up to with that shit stain she considered a boyfriend, and there was no way in hell her own daughter needed to see her like that.

"Well hello to you too, big brother."

I turned, giving Marigold a smile I hoped to hell was reassuring. "Head on to your room and get started on that homework, yeah? I'll call in and order a pizza to be delivered for dinner."

She beamed up at me, raising onto her tip-toes to plant a kiss on my cheek. "All right, Unka, thanks. Love you."

"Love you too, Goldie. Call or text any time. Day or night."

With one last wave to me and without so much as a glance in her mother's direction, she moved through the dreary living room and down the hall. I listened until I heard the door to her bedroom open and close before I turned back to my sister. I barely recognized the woman sitting in front of me just then. At some point, she'd died her brown hair an unflattering platinum blonde. The strands looking like they'd been fried beyond help and there was at least an inch of dark roots at the crown, making it look even worse.

"What the fuck, Angie?" I barked, the bass in my voice making her back shoot straight. She finally forced her gaze off the television that had been playing and looked at me. At least she looked clear-eyed, meaning she probably hadn't gotten around to taking whatever that fucker had supplied her.

Her brows sank down into a frown, the wrinkles between her eyes making her look older than she was. "Jeez, what the hell's your problem?"

My chin jerked back and my jaw dropped in complete shock. "What's my problem?" I asked in bewilderment. "Fuck's sake, where is your goddamn head right now, huh? 'Cause it sure as hell isn't where it should be, that being *on your daughter!*" I ended on a bellow.

"What I do with my daughter is none of your damn business."

"Are you kidding me? Christ, Angie, it is when she calls me in tears because you forgot to pick her up from school a-fucking-gain. Do you even know what time it is? She'd have been out there for hours if she hadn't have been able to reach me. Anything could have happened to her, all because you'd rather spend time with that shithead I saw walking out of here instead of taking care of her."

She flopped back against the couch, crossing her arms over her chest in that pout that used to work when she was a kid but just made her look ridiculous now—not that it ever stopped her. "Jeff's not a shithead."

My head fell back on a bark of caustic laughter. "You can't be serious right now. Out of everything I just said *that's* what jumped out at you? Get your goddamn priorities in line, Ang."

My sister shot off the couch and came toe-to-toe with me, jabbing her finger in my chest. "Don't you tell me how to raise my girl. She's *my* kid, and what I do or don't do is none of your damn business!"

I reined in my temper, hard as it was to do, and managed to lower my voice so Marigold couldn't overhear. I also kept my ears peeled for any signs that she had snuck out of her room and was attempting to eavesdrop. My girl was smart as a whip and sharp as a tack, she knew her mom was worthless, but there was a difference in knowing something and actually hearing it from your parents' mouth that they couldn't be bothered to make time for you.

"It becomes my business when it's obvious you can't be bothered to take care of *your kid*," I stressed, throwing her words back at her. "For fuck's sake, Ang, school got out more than three hours ago. Did you even realize you'd completely forgotten to pick her up before we got here?"

She waved me off and moved back to the couch, picking up the remote to turn the volume up on the television. "She survived just fine, didn't she?"

Her utter lack of concern caused something to snap inside me. The control I'd been struggling so hard to hold onto slipped from my grip. Wrenching the remote out of my sister's hand, I launched the goddamn thing across the house, sending it crashing into the wall and smashing into pieces, rendering it useless.

"What the hell?" Angela yelped, her eyes wide with rage and more than a hint of trepidation. I might not have been a good man, but my father raised me to never lose my cool with a woman. To say what had just happened was out of character would have been a serious understatement. However, I was willing to give myself a little grace, because that loss of control only came due to my worry over Marigold's welfare

"Let's get one thing straight, I'm done with your bullshit." I held up my hand to silence her when she tried to speak. "That means you won't be getting a dime from me when you call whining about being low on cash. I'm done bailing your ass out. If you need money, get a goddamn job. Dad raised you to be a spoiled fuckin' princess, but that shit stopped being cute around the time you got your braces off. He's not here anymore to deal with your bullshit, and I'm done doing it. Grow the fuck up, Angie."

She moved onto the second tool in her arsenal that she used to manipulate everyone around her. Her chin quivered and her eyes grew misty, unfortunately for her, I was immune. "You have no right to throw Dad in my face. You don't know how it's been for me since he died."

I could feel the pulsing of a migraine starting behind my eyeballs. "You're not the only one who lost him, Ang. I lost him, too. Hell, so did Goldie. But that's not an excuse to turn into a leech, sucking everyone else around you dry. I've sat back long enough while you've neglected that girl in there, and I'm telling you right now, it's over."

Her eyes flashed with ire. This conversation wasn't going the way she wanted—meaning she wasn't getting her way—and it was pissing her off. "Is that a threat?" she hissed, glaring daggers in my direction.

"You're goddamn right it is."

She slowly rose to her feet, planting her hands on her hips like she was gearing up for a fight. "You know what? The rest of this god forsaken town might be scared of you and that stupid club, but I'm not. What are you gonna do, huh? Not a damn thing, that's what."

She just overshot her hand and she knew it the second I gave her the same smile I had that skid mark boyfriend of hers. She might have been blood, but that stopped mattering to me when she treated my niece like a piece of shit. You had to earn loyalty, and as far as I was concerned, she hadn't done shit to earn herself my loyalty. But her daughter would have it until the day I left this spinning rock.

"Last mistake you're gonna make is thinkin' I'm all talk, little sister. That *stupid club*, as you called it, has one hell of an attorney on retainer. An attorney I've already been working with to strip you of all legal rights to that girl back there the moment I tell her to pull the trigger." She sucked in a sharp gasp at the news I'd been going behind her back all this time, building a case to protect Marigold in every way necessary. "You push me, and all it'll take is one phone call. Just one, Ang. Do not underestimate the lengths I will go to to protect my girl, even from her own mother."

Leaning over, I snatched up the orange pill bottle I'd spotted the moment I stepped inside. It was clear from the lack of label on the outside that it wasn't something my sister had gotten from the local pharmacist.

Her eyes went wide, darting between me and that pill bottle. "W-what are you doing?"

Instead of answering, I popped the top off and dumped the contents onto the carpet. She let out a yell as she lunged forward, but she wasn't fast enough. I lifted my foot and brought the thick rubber sole of my boot down on the pills, twisting back and forth to grind them into dust before kicking at the spot to send the powder up in a puff.

"You asshole! You had no right—"

"I hope you got what you needed from that piece of shit earlier, because it's the last time you're gonna see him." I took one step closer and pointed my finger in her face, lowering my voice to a low growl to drive my point home. "And if I find out you start buyin' from anyone else, the hell I'll rain down on you will make you wish you'd never been born. Now nod your head so I know you get me."

Her throat worked on a strained swallow as she nodded, her face having gone white as a sheet.

With that, I turned on the heel of my boot and headed out. I made the call to the local pizza place from my truck as I headed toward the garage. Once that was done, I shot out a text for the guys to meet me at the clubhouse.

I had business to take care of tonight. But once Jeff was taken care of, I'd be free to focus on a certain middle school English teacher I couldn't get out of my head.

TWELVE

LENNON

IT WAS 6:00 on a Friday evening as I stood in the aisle of my new town's local market, looking over the small yet respectable variety of red wines they had to choose from. I'd officially finished my first week as a teacher at Ashland Middle School, and I planned to celebrate with a couple glasses of wine, a nice, long bubble bath, and at least one of the bags of dill pickle-flavored potato chips I'd already thrown into my cart.

The week had its fair share of bumps, but that was to be expected any time a person started something new. By the end of it I was a lot more confident in my ability to do my job. Phoebe had become my designated welcoming committee, taking it upon herself to intro- duce me around to the other teachers, filling me in on all the juicy school gossip, and making sure I had people to sit with at lunch each day. There really was a lot to be said for having friends at work. It sure as hell made the days go faster. The kids had finally warmed up to me also, giving me the opportunity to get to know them and their myriad of personalities.

Not all my students made things easy, but that wasn't a surprise. What did surprise me was how quickly Marigold had become one of my favorites—not that I'd ever admit to having favorites out loud, of course.

All in all, it was a pretty good week, but I was glad it was finally over so I could kick back and relax—and maybe have a chance to try again at the whole furniture shopping thing.

I grabbed a familiar wine bottle from one of the middle shelves and placed it in my cart among my coveted pickle chips, a stack of microwavable dinners, a couple pints of my favorite cookie dough ice cream, and several of those pre-packaged bowls of dried noodles you just added water to and nuked for a few minutes.

After kicking Oliver's ass to the curb, I'd taken a little time to reflect on things and discovered one glaring truth I'd been ignoring the entirety of our relationship.

I hated cooking. *Loathed* it.

If my choices were between a root canal and cooking dinner every night, I'd strap on the laughing gas and hop in that reclining chair voluntarily.

Just like so many other things, I'd pushed my dislike for it to the back of my mind because my ex preferred to have a homecooked meal on the table every evening when he got home from work. The only thing that changed on the weekends was that he expected me to whip up all three meals instead of just one.

Never mind the fact that I worked just as many hours as he did. When I pointed that fact out to him early on in our marriage, he'd given me a condescending laugh and explained that I was "only the receptionist", that I "spent my days answering phones while he did *real work*".

Now I knew that *real work* was a euphemism for drinking scotch in his office with his father, uncle, and males cousins like those assholes were characters on *Mad Men* before sneaking away during his lunch hours to fuck women who weren't me.

I grabbed the handles of my cart and started pushing it toward the register, ready to get out of the store and finally kick off my weekend of relaxation. A weekend where I could sleep in, wear my pajamas all day if I wanted to, and not have to answer to a single living soul. The drive from the market to my house took less than ten minutes—another in the long list of bonuses I was quickly discovering came with small-town living. There was no gridlock or rush hour traffic to compete with in the mornings. In fact, I'd actually had enough time each day before school to stop off at a cute little coffee shop called the Daily Grind for a coffee and pastry, so I started each morning fully caffeinated and raring to go.

Another thing really enjoyed about this whole small-town gig happened just after pulling my car into my driveway and throwing the door open. I was gathering the bags from my trunk when I heard a familiar "Yoo hoo," coming from the house to my left.

I turned and smiled at Esther and Otto, the sweet geriatric couple who lived next door. I'd really lucked out having those guys as neighbors. In fact, everyone I'd met on this block so far had been welcoming, kind—if not a teensy bit intrusive—and all-around good people. I never had that in the city.

It wasn't that my neighbors were jerks, necessarily. I hadn't actually known any of them well enough to make that distinction. But everything ran at a much faster pace, and it just seemed like no one had the time to stop and get to know each other.

Not like here in Ashland.

It had taken less than forty-eight hours for the people living on my cute little street to start knocking on my door with introductions, casseroles, and much-welcomed baskets of homemade muffins. I'd seen that kind of thing in TV shows and movies, but I'd never experienced it in real life.

My block held an eclectic mix of people with a wide range of personalities, each one more interesting than the last.

There was Ms. Hofstetter at the end of the cul-da-sac,

a single woman in her late fifties who was supposedly the head of the Neighborhood Watch—meaning she sat at her front window day in and day out with a pair of binoculars and a pitcher of Mai Tai's so she could "keep an eye on things". Then across the street from me were the Kleins. Darnell worked for a construction company one town over, and Aretha was a stay-at-home mom of four kids—all boys, all under the age of seven and *all* full of so much energy it should be downright criminal. It wasn't unusual to hear Aretha shouting inventive threats at her kids to get them in line. Cory Talloway and his wife Kim lived two houses down to my right and had a fondness for rescuing animals in need. One of those pets just so happened to be a Great Dane named Hank who was missing half of his left ear and had such a large, social personality he'd taken to leap-frogging over the back fence whenever he was let out to go to the bathroom and going from house to house to visit with everyone in the neighborhood. The rumor was that he'd learned to ring the doorbells with his nose. Most people kept treats on hand for him for when he got loose, so I started doing the same. I hadn't had a bell ringing visit from Hank yet, but I was really looking forward to that day coming.

Then there was Esther and Otto. Esther was a retired hairdresser who sold the salon she owned in town so she could spend her days gardening and baking for the people who lived around her. Otto had a career in the navy before retiring, and even though the man was knocking on the door to his mid-seventies, he was still in impressive shape. He and his wife both liked to stay busy, so their yard was always beautiful, their flowerbeds tended, and the cheery yellow siding and white shutters on their house were always power-washed to perfection. The cars in their driveway were washed and waxed regularly by Otto, and there was always a load of clean clothes or sheets air drying on the clothes line in the back yard. I'd been invited in for a glass of tea and shortbread cookies a couple times already, and their house was just as spotless on the outside as it was on the inside, not a speck of dust in sight.

Esther had a knack for dragging people's stories out of them in such a way that you didn't realize it was happening, and as soon as I'd finished sharing about my past, she and Otto had decided to take me right under their wing. They'd never had kids of their own—just wasn't something either of them felt was necessary to have a fulfilling life—yet it almost seemed as if they'd adopted the block as their ragtag little family. They babysat, pet sat, and made homemade chicken soup whenever they heard someone was sick.

They were the designated caregivers for our quiet little street, the mother and father figure—or in the case of the four Klein kids, grandparents—and from what I could tell, they were held in high regard by everyone around. Rightfully so by everything I'd experienced.

I looped the handles of the grocery bags over my forearm, freeing my hand to give them a little wave. "Hey, guys."

Esther rose from the porch swing she'd been lounging on with a paperback and a glass of what looked like lemonade while Otto propped the rake he'd been using to clean up leaves in the yard against the porch railing. He started across the thin stretch of yard between our houses, offering me a warm smile and a "Hey sweetheart," said in that pleasant southern accent of his I liked so much. "You have a good day at school?"

I returned his smile with one of my own as he took the bags from my hands, not surprised in the least that he wouldn't let me carry my own groceries. Otto subscribed to that old school chivalry. I hadn't carried in my own groceries or shopping bags since I moved into the house. He'd also taken to cutting my grass on the days he took care of his own, claiming it was no problem at all to just push the mower a little further.

"I did. Although, I'm glad it's over. I'm exhausted."

Esther joined us then, pressing an affectionate kiss to my cheek and looping her arm through mine and patting my hand. "Oh, you poor thing. I can only imagine. A job like that takes someone special."

"They're good kids." The three of us made our way to my front door. "There are just a lot of them," I explained as I used my key to unlock the door and let us all inside.

Otto headed straight to the kitchen, carrying the bags with him as Esther and I moved at a more sedate pace. She released my arm and started unloading my bags, already having made herself familiar with my kitchen days ago.

"Thanks so much, Otto. You're the best."

The big bear of a man moved to me and gave me a sideways hug before brushing a kiss to the crown of my head. It was more affection than I could remember my own father ever giving me, and I would have been lying if I said I it didn't fill a tiny place inside me that I hadn't even realized was empty until I met these two incredible people.

"Anytime, sweetheart. Gotta get back to rakin'. You ladies stay out of trouble." He moved around the island to his wife, dropping a quick but no less affectionate kiss on her lips before patting her behind. Those two had been together more than forty year, but to watch them together, you would think they were newlyweds. More than once I'd experienced a pang of longing, a wish that I'd had someone in my life to treat me like that, to look at me the way Otto still looked at Esther. Oliver had never given me that. I wasn't sure anyone had. But then I remembered why I was in Ashland in the first place. This was my fresh start, and at least for the time being, I had no room for any kind of romantic entanglements.

It was on that thought that my mind drifted to a Courtland Pope.

Gah! Why couldn't I get that damn man out of my head already? They whole point of our night together had been to scratch an itch. He'd done just that—exquisitely so—but instead of being able to move on from that experience, the damn man was taking up way more real estate in my mind than he should have been.

The vibrator in my nightstand drawer had been getting one hell of a workout, to the point I was worried I was going to blow the damn motor out on the thing. And it still wasn't taking the edge off.

"Oh, honey, this just won't do," Esther said, pulling me out of my thoughts and back into reality. She was standing in front of my open freezer, holding a pint of ice cream and a frozen dinner, a look a disapproval on her face. "You can't live off this stuff. It's terrible for you."

I appreciated her concern. It was nice to have someone in my life who actually gave a shit. "I know, but they're just so convenient. And it's been so nice not having to cook dinner every single night."

The stern look she'd been giving me disappeared, her features softening with understanding as she placed the last of the frozen meals in the freezer and closed the door. "I get that, sweetie, but these things are chock full of sodium." She lifted one of the bowls of dried ramen and gave it a shake to emphasize her point. "Keep eating like this and you'll be on the same diet as Otto and just as grumpy." All of a sudden, her face lit up and she clapped her hands together like she just had the best idea ever. "Tell you what, why don't you come over tonight and I'll make you a nice, home cooked dinner that won't clog your arteries or raise your blood pressure."

I appreciate the offer, Esther, truly, and any other night I'd take you up on a home cooked meal, but I have plans tonight with a bathtub full of bubbles, a good book, and some vino." I plucked the wine bottle off the counter and gave it a shake."

She let out a small, tinkling laugh. "All right, Lennon. That sounds like a lovely evening, and you certainly deserve it. But let's plan on something next week. At least let me feed you one day. It'll put my mind at ease."

"You have a deal, Esther. And if I haven't said it before, I'm so glad I moved in next to you and Otto. You guys have been so incredible."

She came over to me, stopping in front of me and lifting her hand to cradle my cheek gently, much like I thought a mother would. The caress was so sweet, so thoughtful, that it was almost enough to bring tears to my eyes as I leaned deeper into her touch. "Oh, dear. We're so glad it was you who ended up buying this place. You came in and it's like you completed everything. I'm so sorry for all that you've been through, but I'm also happy that things worked out the way they did and brought you to Otto and me."

Oh man, she really was incredible. The more I got to know this woman and my new town and all the new friends I'd made, the more I thought the heartache that I went through with Oliver was worth it if this was the new life it led me to.

Her hand dropped so she could place a kiss on the cheek she'd just been holding. "Now you enjoy that bubble bath and get some rest. We'll talk later, sweetheart."

"Thanks, Esther. You guys have a good night."

"You too. We're right next door, so just holler if you need anything."

I was sure I wouldn't need anything, but it felt damn good to know there were people just a few yards away looking out for me.

THIRTEEN

POPE

WITH ONE LAST turn of my wrench, I dug the heels of my boots into the concrete floor and rolled out from beneath the Cougar I'd spent the better part of the day working on.

"Fuckin' hell!" I barked in a jolt of panic when I spotted Bane standing there, leaned against the quarter panel of the car with a shit eating grin on his face.

"About time, Prez. I thought you were asleep under there."

"Jesus, are you trying to give me a heart attack, shit-head? Next time announce yourself instead of standing there lookin' like a goddamn creeper."

I pushed up to standing, dropping my socket wrench back into the tool box with a loud clank and moving to the sink to scrub my hands clean.

He gave me a shit-eating grin. Using his tongue to

shift the toothpick he was chewing on from one side of his mouth to the other. "Hey, not my fault you're getting up there in age."

I shot him the middle finger, earning a laugh. The asshole was leaning up against my car like he didn't have a care in the world. He wore the garage's blue coveralls with the sleeves tied at his waist, protecting his jeans, but leaving his top half uncovered so his white tank and tattoos were on full displace. He toyed with that goddamn toothpick in his mouth and had his motor-cycle-booted feet crossed casually.

I headed in his direction, snatching the toothpick and tossing it away before lightly smacking him upside his head. "Get the hell off my car."

He chuckled, holding his hands up in surrender. "Okay, okay. I'll stay off your baby," he teased before heading over to an old metal stool by the work bench. "So . . . you wanna know why I'm here?"

I pulled a bottle of water out of the minifridge I had stashed under the counter at my station and sucked it back, wiping the back of my mouth with my hand. "You mean besides doing the job I pay you to do?"

He reached behind his back, producing a manilla folder that he waved proudly in the air. "Just thought you'd want the information I was able to find on your girl. But if you'd rather I got back to oil changes and tire rotations—"

I instantly perked up, tossing the now-empty bottle into the recycling bin nearby. "You found her?"

He scoffed. "I'm insulted you'd even ask. Of course I found her."

I snatched the folder from his hands and started flipping through it as he continued talking. "Got an address, date of birth, social security number. Hell, I even got everything on her husband."

My head shot up and I barely managed to keep from rocking back on my boot as that news slammed into my chest with all the power of a physical blow. My fingers started to curl around the folder and documents in my hands, threatening to crumple them into oblivion.

"She's married?" The jealousy I felt just then wasn't rational. I was aware of that. But I was also keenly aware of the fact that the woman had somehow managed to burrow her way beneath my skin after just one night in a way no one ever had before. I couldn't explain the draw I felt toward her, but I wanted her with the kind of intensity that would have probably scared off most other men. However, everything about the life I'd grown up in was intense, so I wasn't the kind of man to scare off easily. When I wanted something, I went after it, full force. And Christ, but I wanted Lennon Cody. I craved her.

"Was." His focus on me turned scrutinizing. I was usually a hell of a lot better at hiding my reactions. It was something I'd had to learn in my position. I'd gotten really fucking good at not revealing much of anything because there were too many people out there who would happily take my weaknesses and use them against me.

"Her divorce was finalized right before she moved to town." He jerked his chin toward the folder. "There are a couple pics in there I pulled from his social media. Guy looks like a real douchebag if you ask me."

My curiosity got the better of me, and I flipped through the pages until I got to the guy Bane had to be talking about. There was one of him standing on a dock in front of a speed boat, his arms thrown wide, shit eating grin on his face. He wore a pair of swim trunks and an unbuttoned Hawaiian shirt that showed off a lack of muscle definition and a softness in his gut that came from living a pampered lifestyle. The other photo was him in the middle of a green, hanging off a gold cart with a bunch of guys who looked like frat bro assholes. They all had beers in their hands and looked three sheets to the wind.

"Jesus, really? *This* guy?" Bane was right. He was a fucking douche, no doubt about it. And when I pictured Lennon, I couldn't for the life of me put her with a dumbass like this.

"What are we lookin' at?"

I looked up from the folder just as Roe came over to join us.

"Fuckin' hell. Does no one work around here anymore?" I grumbled. He seemed as unbothered by my attitude as Bane did, but I'd expect nothing less from my Vice President.

If Pops was who I went to for guidance, Roe was who I went to for everything else. If I hadn't had him at my back when I was trying to pull my club out of the gutter, I don't think I would have been able to pull it off. Hell, if he hadn't been looking out, I'd most likely be buried six feet deep somewhere with a bullet in the back of my head.

We'd prospected together, climbed the ranks together, and worked side by side to turn the Wraiths into a legacy we'd be happy to pass down. Out of all my brothers, he was the one I was closest to, the one I trusted the most. He was the one person on the planet who knew all my secrets.

"This comin' from the asshole who's been buried under that Mercury all day instead of working on one of the million custom builds we've got goin'?"

He wasn't wrong about that. I had more than enough work I needed to focus on, but I had to be in the right frame of mind in order to do that, and lately, I'd had too much shit spinning around in my head to be able to focus the way I needed to. The Cougar was mine. It was what I worked on when I either needed to clear my head or was trying to work something out on my own, so it didn't matter if I fucked something up.

He snatched the folder from my hand and started skimming through it, a shit-eating grin tugging at the prick's mouth as he paged through the information. "Ah, I see. It's about the fairy princess."

I looked at him, raising my brows in question.

"You know, like all that Disney shit?" Bane took over explaining. All of us who were with you at Toni's that night saw her."

"And she looks just like that one chick . . ." he snapped his fingers, trying to think of the name. "You know. Dark hair. Stepmom's tryin' to murder her. Eats a poison apple."

"Snow White," I supplied, not ashamed in the slightest that I knew that. Thanks to Marigold's fascination with all those movies, I was extremely familiar with all things cartoon Princess.

Roe pointed at me. "That's the one. She looks just like Snow White."

"Only less animated and a lot fuckin' hotter," Bane added, earning a murderous glare from me that had him putting his hands up in surrender.

Roe laughed as he snapped the folder closed and smacked it into my chest. "Shit man. This one's really gotten under your skin, huh? Never seen you hung up like this before. You're usually the first to bounce after getting your dick wet."

"Must have a golden snatch."

Before my brain had a chance to engage, my arm shot out, my hand fisted in the collar of Bane's tank, and I used my hold to jerk him toward me, curling my lips back like an animal as I hissed, "Talk about her like that again and I'll knock every one of your goddamn teeth down your throat. You got me?"

The bastard let out a hearty laugh. "Loud and clear, Prez. Loud and clear."

I shoved him away and pulled in a deep breath, willing myself to calm the hell down. I couldn't go around losing my cool like that.

"All right. Chattin' time's over. Get your ass back to work."

Bane threw me a salute and reached into the pocket of his coveralls, producing a pack of smokes and a lighter. He lit a cigarette as he walked away, whistling a carefree tune.

"Christ," Roe said, his voice holding humor as he shook his head. "That asshole's unflappable."

He usually was. But we knew the truth of what lay behind that unperturbed façade. Bane was always the picture of calm. Until he wasn't. It took a hell of a lot to get him to snap, but when he did, he went from calm to psycho faster than the speed of sound. You didn't want to be anywhere near when he lost his shit. Truthfully, the few times I'd witnessed it had left a little unsettled and more than happy he was on our side.

Back in the day, he used to be our best fighter. He'd raked in more money with our underground fighting ring than all the other guys combined. But there was a reason no one would fight him anymore. He was more than happy to spend his days working and his nights partying and fucking his way through the female population of Ashland. But when we needed him, he was just fine being let off that leash.

"She's a looker, brother, I'll give you that. But you really gonna get yourself tangled up in some woman right now? You think that's smart?"

Roe's question pulled my mind back to the present and my focus to him. "There somethin' wrong with the timing? The club's in a good place. We're solid financially, and the past has been dealt with."

He lifted a brow at me. "Not all of it," he replied ominously.

My face fell into a frown, my lips tensing in a straight line. "That's settled. There's no sense in bringing it up."

"Is it, though?" he pushed. "The rumors are still floating around, and you know it. What if she hears the stories."

"Then I'll tell her the same thing we've been tellin' everyone for years. The club had nothing to do with it."

He crossed his arms over his chest, his expression inscrutable. "You say that now, but what if you get in deep with this chick, Pope? I'm tellin' you right now, that happens, lyin' to her isn't gonna feel real good."

"It'll be fine."

"And if it's not?"

"Then I'll deal," I snapped, slamming my palm down on the hood of the Cougar.

"You say that like it's easy." He shook his head like he disapproved. "There are only four people still breathin' who know the truth, Pope. The *actual* truth. And two of them are standin' right here. We've kept this secret all these years because we know what's at stake. That shit comes out and people could end up hurt. Or worse."

"You think I don't know that?" I gritted out. I wasn't a big fan of having my judgment put into question. "I'm the one who made the fuckin' call in the first place, who put that shit into action."

Roe let out a heavy sigh, like the weight of the world was resting on his shoulders. I got it. Truly. I carried that very same weight. Usually I had my club to lean on, but Roe and I had agreed that what had gone down all those years ago was best kept quiet. The fewer people who knew, the better. This was just another in a long line of secrets I intended to take with me to the grave. My father had taken his fair share with him, but hopefully the work I'd done to pull us out of the shit would prevent future generations from carrying that same burden.

"All right, Prez. You know you got my trust. I'll drop it."

The knot that had started to form in my chest loosened, making it possible to pull in a full breath. I didn't care to think about that particular time in my life. It was something best kept buried, and now that Roe had agreed to let it go, I intended to shove it six feet down again and smother it with dirt where it belonged.

"Good. Now if you don't mind, I got shit to do."

Roe's easy humor returned as I pushed past him, heading for the office. "Oh, I bet you do. I'll tell the rest of the guys not to expect you at the bar tonight."

I shot a two finger salute over my shoulder, not bothering to turn back because he was right. I planned on being way too busy to meet up with them later."

FOURTEEN

POPE

I GUIDED my bike along the tree-lined street, taking in Lennon's cozy neighborhood. It wasn't one of those newer cookie-cutter developments where every other house looked the exact same. The houses were older, but they were well maintained, each having character of its own.

The sun was starting to lower in the sky, creating a dappled glow of orange that broke through the canopy of leaves and branches that stretched over the road. The engine of my bike sounded so much louder than normal against the quiet block. I wouldn't have been surprised if people had moved to their front windows to get a look at who was passing by. Though I was sure they were all familiar with the patch I was currently wearing. The Iron Wraiths were well known in this town. For good reasons and bad. We'd been here a long time.

I turned into Lennon's driveway, stopping behind the SUV already parked there, and killed the engine, I pushed the kickstand down as I unbuckled the chin strap of my beanie helmet an lifted it off while taking her place in. The little bungalow suited her somehow, and it didn't take any effort to picture her moving around inside. The hedges along the front porch had been trimmed back, the lawn was freshly cut, and I found myself wondering if she'd been out here taking care of that stuff herself, or if she hired someone to take care of it.

It wasn't lost on me that what little I knew about the woman I'd been inside of multiple times over the course of less than twelve hours was what my guy had managed to find online through a few less than legal channels. I wanted to know more. Hell, I wanted to know everything. From the most prominent color hanging in her closet to her favorite food and everything between.

That was why I was here. Well, that, and because I was desperate to get inside her again. And that was exactly what it was, a desperation.

"'Scuze me." I turned my head at the sound of the voice and saw an older man starting across the yard of the cheery house next door. I pushed up, lifting my leg over the bike, and rose to my full height just as he stepped onto the concrete pad that made up Lennon's driveway. "Can I help you?"

I pulled my shades off and sat them on the back of the bike by my helmet before giving the dude a long, assessing look. The skin on his face was weathered and lined with age, and the hair on his head and eyebrows was a deep steel gray. If I had to guess, I'd have put him somewhere in his seventies, but even at that age, he was stocky as fuck. His gaze was shrewd and his mouth was pulled in a tight line as he took me in the same as I'd just done to him. He had his feet braced shoulder-width apart, arms crossed over his chest, and I got the distinct impression he was on alert, ready to move at any second. I'd gotten pretty damn good at reading people over the years, and I was willing to bet this guy was either former military or law enforcement of some kind. Though I was leaning more toward the first.

"Don't think so," I answered, lifting my brows in curiosity.

Just then, a woman around the same age stepped out onto the wrap-around porch of the yellow house. "Everything okay, Otto?"

The man—now known as Otto—didn't take his eyes off me as he answered his wife. "Not sure yet." Then to me he said, "Look, son, I mean no offense, but I know what that patch you're wearin' means. Been here a long time, and I've heard the stories. You could very well be a decent enough guy, but that girl in there's been through hell, and if you're here to lay anymore on her doorstep,

I'm gonna have to ask you to leave. She deserves a break."

Usually I *would* have taken offense to something like this, but as I stared at the guy, I had to give him credit for not backing down. He didn't seemed phased by my scrutiny one damn bit. Whoever this man was, he'd seen some shit, and it had made him tough as a brick shithouse. I actually liked the fact Lennon had someone like him looking out for her. He really was concerned about her wellbeing, and instead of getting pissed for his snap judgement of me and my club—whether or not it was deserved—I found myself appreciating the fact that the raven-haired beauty inside had people watching out for her best interests.

I was also more than a little curious about this past he was alluding to. Did the nightmare he spoke of have to do with her ex? Was that golf-shirt wearing shithead giving her a hard time? Part of me hoped the answer was yes so I could take care of it for her.

"Otto, what's going on? Who is that man?" the woman called.

At her question, I decided I'd been silent long enough. "Look, man. I'm not here to cause any trouble. Lennon and I are . . . friends."

The woman next door called out again. "What's he saying?"

Before the guy could answer his curious wife, the front door to Lennon's house swung open, and the object of every dirty thought I'd had while jerking my own dick over the past couple weeks stepped out, looking like a goddamn wet dream.

That mass of ebony hair was piled high on the top of her head with tendrils that had escaped the clip holding it all up hanging down and caressing her neck and temples. Her skin was flushed and dewy, like she'd just climbed out of the shower, and her long legs were on display thanks to the short silk robe she was wearing that left little to the imagine.

One arm was wrapped protectively across her chest while the other hand held the lapels of the robe tight at her throat for a bit more modesty.

"Otto, is everything okay? I heard voices—" Her words died and those sea foam eyes widened as soon as they landed on me.

I couldn't help the wicked grin that tugged at my lips as I let my gaze caress her from the tips of her bubblegum pink toes to that bun I wanted to grip onto as I drove my cock into her from behind.

Fuck, she looked good. She looked hot as hell that night at the bar. When I saw her at the middle school she looked sweet and sexy. But right at that moment, with her face completely bare of makeup and that flimsy robe the only thing masking her delectable curves, she took my goddamn breath away.

"Hey there, Raven."

Her lips parted, her mouth dropping open in shock, and it took everything in me not to reach out and yank her to me so I could seal my lips over hers.

"Uh . . ."

"Lennon, sweetie, you know this guy?"

The apples of her creamy pale cheeks burned pink under her neighbors' attention. "He's . . . a friend."

I grinned widely, turning back to Otto who still didn't seem convinced. "See? Told you?"

"Ooh, dear." The woman next door tugged at the collar of her shirt like she was fanning herself and waggled her eyebrows at Lennon. "He's quite the looker, sweetie. *Very* handsome."

Otto rolled his eyes on a beleaguered groan as he dropped his hands at his sides. "Christ's sake Esther."

"Oh, don't you start," the woman chided. "I'm married, not blind or dead. And you know I think you're handsome too or I wouldn't put up with your grumpy behind."

I barely managed to keep from chuckling as Lennon drew closer, embarrassment tinging her cheeks and the tips of her ears a deep red as she mumbled, "Oh my god."

"Just so you know, sweetie, I approve." Esther threw both thumbs up our way, and that seemed to be all my Raven could take.

She reached out and grabbed my arm, giving it a tug in the direction of the house. "Thanks, Esther, but we're just friends."

I looked to the woman practically hanging over her porch railing and winged my brows upward as I rumbled, "For now."

That had the desired effect, causing Esther's cheeks to flush as she let out a little giggle. I didn't think I was the best looking guy on the planet, but I knew the appeal I had, and I knew exactly how to use it. And I'd just made sure I won Ether over to my side.

"Stop talking and get *inside*," Lennon hissed under her breath as she continued to pull at me until I unplanted my boots and finally started to move.

She walked backwards, trailing behind me a few steps as she gave the older couple an awkward wave. "See you guys later. Have a good night. I'll talk to you tomorrow," she rambled. As soon as my boot hit the front porch, she whipped around and all but shoved me across the threshold and into her house, following right behind me and slamming the door shut. "What the hell?" she cried. "Why would you say that? Now they think we're sleeping together."

"We did sleep together," I answered as I turned in a slow circle, taking everything in. I wasn't sure what I'd been expecting when it came to her place, but it sure as hell hadn't been this.

Aside from a single loveseat, there wasn't any other furniture in the living room. She didn't even have a stand for her TV. The television was against the opposite wall, sitting on a stack of moving boxes. There weren't any personal touches either, no photos, or wall art, nothing.

"*Are* and *did* mean two completely different things, Pope," she said in a scolding tone, the English teacher in her coming out, and I wasn't mad at it. In fact, if she threw on a pair of glasses and some heels just then, she'd be living out a fantasy I'd had since I learned the jerk off. "We *did* sleep together. But we aren't anymore. We talked about this."

I turned back to her and smiled, taking in the crossed arms and cocked hip as she frowned in my direction. "We started talking about it, but that conversation is far from finished." I took a step closer to her, reaching out to tuck one of the locks of hair that had fallen loose behind her ear. I didn't miss the way her breath hitched and her eyes glazed over, or the frantic flutter of the pulse in her neck as I closed in. Christ, she smelled good. Like a warm island breeze on a bright, sunny day. The scent of coconut and oranges on her skin made me want to lean in and run my tongue across that pulse in her throat to see if she tasted as sweet as she smelled.

I opened my mouth to tell her just how badly I wanted her, only to be interrupted by the sharp, tinny sound of her doorbell.

I pulled back, my brows shooting together in a frown. "You expectin' company tonight, darlin'?"

She tipped her head slightly to the side and looked at the door in confusion. "No. I was supposed to have a quiet night in. Maybe it's Otto and Esther?"

Otto's words from earlier rang in my head. I still didn't know what type of nightmare Lennon had lived through, but I wasn't about to take any risks. Placing my hand on her stomach, I guided her back and behind me."

Her brows furrowed and she hit me with as hard look as I moved toward the door. "What are you doing?"

"Just stay behind me," I ordered as I looked through the peep-hole. The bell rang again, but there was no one on the other side. "What the hell?"

I felt her move in close, those fantastic tits I'd spent hours tasting pressing into my back as she raised up on her toes to try and get a peek. "Who is it?" she whispered.

"There's no one there. Must be a short in the bell or something." I reached for the knob, and the moment I twisted it, something on the other side gave a mighty push, nearly shoving me out of the way. "What the fuck?" I barked as an animal the size of a small horse shoved its way into Lennon's house.

My head whipped around on her sharp gasp, and my confusion only grew at the sight of her excitement. She stood a few feet away, her hands clasped at her chest and the biggest, brightest smile on her face as she bounced up and down on the balls of her feet.

"Oh my god, he finally came," she said in awe, opening her arms and crouching down like she wanted to hug the thing.

I cut in front of her, shoving her back as I stared at something that looked like it was supposed to be a dog. "Jesus, don't get close to it," I snapped. "It could be aggressive . . ." I looked it the mangled ear on the left side of its head . . . "or sick."

"Oh stop it." She shot me a glower as she shoved past me to get closer to the dog, dropping down to her knees and wrapping her arms around it's long, thick neck. "This is Hank, and there's absolutely nothing wrong with him." She pulled back, her expression going dreamy as she babytalked, "Is there? No there isn't. Who's a good boy for using the doorbell? Who's a good boy?"

The dog, Hank—who the hell named a dog *Hank,* for Christ's sake—plopped down on his ass, his long tail swishing back and forth across the floor like an eager broom as he lapped up the attention.

"Raven, you wanna tell me what the hell's goin' on and why you have a goddamn *dog* ringin' your door bell?"

She rose to her feet on a giggle and moved toward the kitchen, leaving the door standing wide open. Hank and I followed after her voice as she explained, "That's Hank. He lives two doors down and is a bit of an escape artist." She pulled a bag of dog treats from one of the cabinets and ripped open the seal. "Apparently he's just too social to stay cooped up and likes to roam the neighborhood from time to time visiting everyone."

"And the doorbell trick?"

"Self-taught," she said proudly as she rounded the island, a few dogs treats in her hand for Hank. "Or at least that's how the story goes. Everyone keeps treats on hand for when he decides to visit. I've been waiting and waiting, and here he is, *finally*," she finished, her tone downright giddy. And I had to admit, it was funny as hell. A dog who got out so he could visit his neighbors, ringing doorbells all over the block for treats. He had his game down pat, that was for damn sure.

He gobbled down the treats, then turned on his giant feet and clomped right back out the door.

"Bye, Hank!" Lennon called, like the dog could actually understand. "See you next time."

I looked back to the woman who was watching after the dog like that little visit just made her whole week. And it hit me like a bolt of lightning. This woman fascinated me in a way I'd never experienced before, and I'd be damned if I was letting her get away.

Not when I'd only just found her.

FIFTEEN

LENNON

WITHOUT THE DRAMA of my neighbors and the gigantic buffer that had been Hank, I was suddenly very aware of the fact that Courtland Pope was standing in my house. He was looking at me like I was a prime rib and he'd been starving for the better part of the week, and it would have been a lie if I said a thrill didn't run through me at the way those black coffee eyes of his scanned me from head to toe.

A breeze traveled in through the open door blowing across my bare legs and reminding me that I was wearing nothing more than a short, flimsy robe. *Shit.*

Snatching the lapels, I bunched them together to cover myself more and began backing away toward the hall that led to my bedroom. "Um . . ." I threw my thumb over my shoulder right before I bumped into the wall.

"I'm just going to throw something on real quick. Be right back."

Before he could say a word, I whipped around and skittered down the hall. I slammed the door closed and collapsed against it, dropping my head back and banging it lightly against the wood as I tried to unravel my tangled thoughts.

I should have been asking questions like what was he doing here and how did he find out where I live, but I was too busy trying to calm my body's reaction to the sight of him to think rationally. In my defense, I'd been in the middle of a very promising solo sesh when the voices coming from outside interrupted my impending release.

Moving to the suitcase I had sitting open in the middle of my closet floor—because it wasn't only furniture I'd yet to buy, but also hangers and dishes, and basically anything a human being needed to live comfortably —I fished through the clothes in there, tossing things aside until I landed on a pair of leggings and my favorite tee—a faded Led Zeppelin t-shirt that I'd stolen from my father years and years ago and cut up so the sleeves were shorter and it was cropped at my belly button.

I rushed to the bathroom, pausing momentarily to look longingly at the full tub I'd been soaking in before I had to climb out to see what the hell was going on outside. The bottle of wine was sitting on the floor beside the half full glass and my Kindle. I'd abandoned my book, trading it in for my waterproof vibrator when the particularly spicy scene I'd been reading had gotten me all hot and bothered. When the image of the hero I'd been envisioning changed to Pope, I'd had no choice but to try and relieve a bit of pressure or I wouldn't have been able to get a damn thing done.

"No, Lennon," I scolded quietly when my mind began to wander again my body went along for the ride. I moved to the mirror and stripped off my robe, glaring at my hard nipples. The damn things were throbbing and pointed sharp enough to cut glass "Stupid nipples. Get your shit together. It was *one night.* It isn't happening again."

A tiny voice in the back of my head spoke up then, asking *but why? It was so damn fun.*

I ignored it and dressed quickly, skipping a bra and panties in my rush to get back out there. It was because I wanted to know what he was doing in my home, I told myself. *Not* because I was excited by the fact I got to see him again.

I padded down the hall on bare feet, expecting to see him in the living room since it had the only place to sit, but instead, I found him in the kitchen, standing in front of my opened fridge. "Uh. What are you doing?"

He pushed the fridge shut and turned toward me, a look of bewilderment on his face. "Raven, what the hell?

You don't have any food. How the hell do you live like this?"

My brows lowered in offense as I declared, "I have food," and moved into the kitchen, brushing past him and whipping the door to the freezer open. "See?"

His features fell into a flat expression that almost made me laugh. "That shit's not real food. You can't live off that stuff."

I crossed my arms over my chest protectively. "I don't intend to. I'm also quickly accumulating menus from all the restaurants in town that deliver, thank you very much."

He held his hands up, reading the tightness in my tone. "Sorry, darlin'. Didn't mean any offense. It's no big deal if you can't cook."

"I *can* cook," I said, the need to defend myself growing stronger by the second. "Quite well, as a matter of fact. I just don't like to."

Something in his features shifted. His face softened and those dark eyes warmed as he leaned his hips back against the counter across from me, crossing one booted ankle over the other. He was the picture of comfort, like he'd been in my house a million times and had no issues making himself at home. And for some crazy reason, I didn't mind the sight of him here. "This have anything to do with your dickhead ex?"

My jaw dropped and my eyes threatened to bug out of my skull. "How . . . how do you know about that?"

His smile was almost wicked. "I have my ways."

Why wasn't I surprised. "I see. I guess that's how you also managed to get my address without me giving it to you?"

"Yep." He didn't appear the slightest bit ashamed at having used whatever means he had at his disposal to invade my privacy. I probably should have been more upset about it; in fact, I was trying my hardest to work up a good mad, but it wasn't happening. That small piece of me that had hoped to see him again after our night together was thrilled he'd managed to track me down, even if he'd gone about it in a creepy, stalker-y way.

Dear Lord, what the hell is wrong with me?

I had more than enough experience spotting warning signs from a great distance, and this dude was a walking red flag. I must be losing my freaking mind, because for some reason I *liked* it. It wasn't the same as it had been with Oliver, where I'd ignored all the signs and hoped things would get better. This time I saw them clear as day. I just didn't care.

Which was even more of a reason to stay away from this guy. I had a nasty habit of being so desperate for someone to love me, to choose me, that I tended to lose myself completely when it came to the men in my life. With my father, I was so starved for his affection that I did anything I could for his approval. I cleaned, I cooked, I did the laundry. I made sure I always did my homework, got straight As, and never got in trouble at school because I didn't want to be the cause of any stress or disappointment. Not that he ever cared enough to notice. With Oliver, I became the version of Lennon that *he* wanted me to be.

After the divorce was finalized I began to wonder if I'd ever made a decision based on what *I* wanted. I couldn't go down that road again. I was still trying to find myself, to learn what I liked and what I didn't. I wouldn't allow myself to get sucked up in another man.

Heaving out a sigh, I figured it was best to get right to the point, rip the Band-Aid off quickly. "Yes. It's because of my dickhead ex."

His brows winged upward, clearly surprised that I had answered honestly. Then his features grew hard and cold, like they'd been carved from a giant slab of marble. "He also the reason you're livin' like a squatter without a damn bit of furniture?"

"Yes. But not like you're thinking?" He waited silently for me to explain. I let out a gust of air and threw my hands up before carrying on. "I just wanted out. After I found out he'd cheated on me multiple times with multiple women—one of whom was *supposed* to be my friend—I wanted to get divorced and move on.

So to make things easier, I didn't fight him for anything."

Pope's face fell, his features softening with compassion. "Jesus, baby." I told myself that hearing him call me baby wasn't the reason for the zing I felt shoot through my body before centralizing in my core. That the low, gravelly rumble of his voice didn't make my nerves fire like I was holding on to a fallen powerline.

"I hated all the furniture in the house we shared together. I didn't realize it when I lived there, but looking back, it was uncomfortable and overly fussy. I didn't want any of it. I didn't want the house. I sure as hell didn't want the bed we'd shared, so I let him keep it all."

Pope moved closer and it took everything in me not to get lost in those deep, fathomless eyes. "You didn't want anything from your old life?"

The smell of wind and leather and spice invaded my senses, causing heat to build low in my belly. I shook my head and lowered my voice. "None of it was me. I might have made myself believe it had been what I wanted while his mother was dragging me from store to store and basically forcing her opinion on me, but after I kicked him out, when I finally stopped to look around, I realized there wasn't a single piece of me anywhere in there. It was like I didn't exist inside those four walls. So I walked away from everything, and I'm not sad about it."

He reached up, dragging the tips of his fingers across my jawline and down my neck, eliciting a full body shiver from me. God, everything about this man was just so . . . *potent*. It wasn't just his impressive height of the hard body packed with muscles. It was his presence. Everything about it was so damn big and overwhelming. He was the type of man you could easily lose yourself in, and if I wasn't careful, he'd consume me.

"What about now?" he asked in that quiet, raspy voice. "You finding yourself in these four walls?"

I wanted him to keep touching me, to slide those work-rough hands down my body and slip them beneath the thin barrier of my clothes so I could feel him skin-on-skin.

But just because I wanted something didn't mean I could have it.

"I'm still working on it," I answered honestly, taking a step back and ignoring the sudden wave of cold that made me shiver at the loss of his touch. Three times. I'd been in this man's presence *three times*, and my body was already reacting like I was addicted. I had to put a stop to this. Whether I wanted to or not.

"Which is why this"—I waved my hand in the space between us—"isn't a good idea. I just got out of a relationship, Pope. It might have been toxic, and ending it might be the best decision I ever made, but it was a very big, very important part of my life, and I need to figure out what the hell I'm doing before I can think about starting something up with someone else."

Or you could just say screw it and climb the man like a koala, that stupid voice piped in.

My breath hitched when he moved closer, bracing his hands on the counter behind me, on either side of my hips, and caging me in. *God,* he smelled so good! I didn't think I'd ever wanted a man so badly; my desire was a visceral, living, breathing thing, clawing beneath my skin and setting my blood on fire.

"Do you want me?"

My breath hitched as my gaze darted between his tantalizing lips and those deep eyes. "It's not that simple."

He lowered his head, dragging the tip of his nose along the column of my neck and breathing deeply like he was trying to fill his lungs with my scent. I had to lock my knees to keep myself from swaying closer to him.

"Oh, it absolutely is that simple, Raven. See, what I've been hearing is that you spent years putting your wants aside for someone else." He moved one hand, bringing it to my waist so he could drag the tips of his fingers along the few inches of bare stomach between my leggings and shirt. I curled my lips between my teeth to stop the whimper that wanted to escape as my eyes fell closed. "Don't you think it's time you do something for yourself?"

He was suddenly making so much sense. The more he talked, the more he touched me, the harder it was to remember the laundry list of reasons why we should stay away from each other. I nodded my head, unable to speak past the dryness in my throat. My hands trembled as I fisted the front of his shirt to stay upright.

He pulled back just enough for his gaze to lock with mine, and suddenly I felt like I was treading water in the middle of the ocean beneath the midnight sky. He was all I could see, our lips only inches apart. So close all I had to do was lean in and I'd be kissing him. And *God*, I wanted to kiss him.

"So tell me, what do you want?"

The answer really was as simple as he claimed.

"You," I said on a hushed breath. "I want you."

SIXTEEN

LENNON

APPARENTLY THE MAN had been holding himself back with an iron grip on his control, because once those words passed my lips, that tether snapped. On a growl, Pope's mouth crashed down onto mine, his tongue probing and demanding entry.

The instant my lips parted, his tongue swirled with mine, and just like that, my brain short-circuited. All I could think about was him. He was everywhere, invading every one of my senses, and I didn't mind one damn bit.

He swallowed down my whimper as I looped my arms around his neck, desperately trying to get closer, our mouths feeding from one another in a ravenous kiss that made my knees weak. I'd never been kissed like that in my life, like he was frantic for it, like he couldn't get enough of me and was desperate for more.

His strong arm banded around my waist, holding me tight against the ridged plane of his chest and lifting me up so I was on my tiptoes. My fingers dug into the hair at the back of his head, fisting the long strands as his hand came up and removed the clip that held my hair back. His fingers tangled in my long locks as they fell around my shoulders, his grip tight enough to make my scalp sting deliciously as he tipped my head to the angle he wanted.

He dominated every aspect of that kiss, building this fire inside me that threatened to burn me alive. He didn't handle me with care as he pinned me to the counter, rocking his hips against me so I could feel the evidence of his desire pressing like a steel rod into my belly. He wasn't soft or gentle as he ripped his mouth from mine and trailed stinging, biting kisses along my neck and collarbone, no doubt leaving marks in his wake.

Even if we hadn't had that one night together already, I could tell by the way his mouth was devouring me he wasn't the kind of guy to stick with missionary that lasted all of ten minutes three times a week, then would roll over and pass out as soon as he got off. Sex wasn't routine for a man like Courtland Pope. It was a battle, a fucking Olympic event in which he wouldn't settle for anything other than gold.

This man was the Michael freaking Phelps of sex, and I kicked myself for fighting it.

I moaned into his mouth when his large hand skated beneath the hem of my T-shirt and slid up to grab my breast. He wasn't gentle with that either. The second his fingers found my nipple, they pinched hard, making it throb as a wave of arousal flooded my core, soaking my leggings between my thighs.

"You like that, Raven?" he asked before raking his teeth across the sensitive skin at my neck and sucking right over where my pulse thrummed wildly. He ground his cock against me as he palmed my breast, squeezing and plumping it until my nipple pulsed in time with my clit. Then he moved to the other to give it the same attention. "You like it when I'm rough with you?"

I absolutely did. It was what I'd craved with Oliver, but what he'd held back our entire marriage, choosing to give that part of himself to other women instead of me.

"Yes," I panted, my head falling back to give Pope better access. "More." Apparently the man had fried my brain so I was only capable of speaking one word at a time.

He pulled back, his wide chest rising and falling with ragged breaths like he'd just run a marathon, his eyes like deep pools of molten hot oil about to catch fire. "Do you have any fuckin' clue how badly I've wanted you?" he asked on a ferocious growl. "Christ, you've been driving me out of my goddamn mind. I feel like I should punish you for walkin' out on me that morning and makin' me wait all this time for another taste."

A switch suddenly flipped inside me and I went from turned on to desperate faster than I could blink. "Do it," I said, those two words falling past my lips as soon as he finished his statement.

His nostrils flared, surprise flashing in his gaze.

"Do it, Pope," I repeated, my heart lurching in my chest, beating against my ribs.

A wicked, greedy smile curled his lips upward and sent a shiver through my entire body. "You want me to punish you, baby?"

My throat worked on a swallow as I nodded. "I want you to do whatever you want to me."

God, who *was* I?

I didn't know when the hell I'd become so bold, but I liked it.

His lips curled back from his teeth, his expression turning positively feral as his arm lashed out and his hand grasped me by my throat, squeezing gently. The grip wasn't to scare me, and I knew that without question. It was commanding, possessive, and it made my body light up like the night sky on Independence Day.

He brought his face so close the tip of his nose brushed against mine. "Just remember, Lennon; you asked for it."

Hell, I'd practically begged for it. And I didn't feel an

ounce of shame or embarrassment over it. He had been right. It was high time I started demanding what *I* wanted. That was what I'd done the night I met this man, and that was the most fun I'd had in too damn long. I wanted more of that. And why the hell shouldn't I have it?

I let out a startled yelp that quickly morphed into a giggle when Pope grabbed hold of me and flung me over his shoulder in a fireman's hold like I weighed next to nothing. His boots clomped against my hardwood floors as he lumbered down the hall toward my bedroom.

"Thank fuck," he grunted under his breath once we crossed the threshold. "At least you have a bed."

I was pretty freaking thankful about that myself. He slowly lowered me to my feet, making sure to drag me down the front of his body so I could feel that erection still straining to be let loose. "You ready for your punishment?"

Boy, was I ever. I nodded silently, pulling my bottom lip between my teeth and biting down.

"Strip," he ordered, that one-word command coming out harsh and abrasive, like he was teetering on the very edge of his control.

I did as he said, but took my time, teasing and drawing it out as I slipped out of my shirt and lowered my leggings down to my ankles before stepping out of them, revealing that I hadn't been wearing anything underneath.

"Mm," he hummed approvingly. "My dirty girl. You haven't been wearing any panties this whole time?"

I bit the inside of my cheek, a smile tugging at my lips as I shook my head.

He moved into me, dragging the tip of his nose along my neck and breathing deeply. "Christ, I can smell how turned on you are. Smells like fuckin' heaven." My chest hitched on a stuttered breath. He wasn't even touching me, but I felt like I was about to combust. "Are you wet for me, Lennon?" He pulled back, reaching up to twirl a lock of my hair around his index finger. "Bet you're drenched. Bet that hot pussy of yours is throbbing for me."

"Pope," I said on a whimper as the heartbeat between my thighs picked up the pace.

"Get on the bed. Spread those pretty thighs wide and show me how soaked you are."

I lowered to the edge of the mattress and pushed myself backward until I was in the center of the bed. He stood at the foot, still fully dressed, with his feet braced shoulder-width apart and his arms crossed as his gaze caressed my body. It wasn't lost on me that he was still fully clothed while I was totally naked and stretched out for his pursual. But as I leaned back on my elbows and planted my feet in the bed, letting my bent knees fall open so he could see the most intimate part of me, I felt more powerful than I ever had in my whole life.

A low, raspy sound rumbled from deep within his chest as his eyes locked on to my center. If I wasn't watching so closely, I might have thought he was completely unaffected, but I didn't miss the way his tongue darted out, tracing over his plump bottom lip as his Adam's apple bobbed on a thick swallow, or the clench of his fists.

I was so aroused that the slight breeze from the air conditioner across my wet slit was enough to make my entire body tremble. I was on tenterhooks. One touch was liable to set me off, but Pope wasn't coming any closer.

"Such a pretty pussy," he said in a low rasp. "Drenched and swollen. Touch yourself, Lennon. Slide a finger inside so I can see exactly how wet you are.

I licked my lips, my mouth suddenly feeling dry as I pushed myself up on one hand and slid the other down my belly. My whole body quaked as I grew closer, and when I dipped my middle finger inside, my eyes fell shut and my head drooped back on a needy moan.

"That feel good?"

"So good," I said on a gust of breath, pulling my finger out and sliding it back in, growing impossibly wetter.

"Ah, ah, ah. I didn't say to fuck yourself. I said show

me." I blinked my eyes open, my vision hazy as I took him in, standing so big and proud at the foot of my bed. "Take it out and let me see." My bottom lip poked out in a pout, but I did as he said, earning a pleased hum from him when he saw how the digit glistened with my arousal beneath my bedroom lights. "Now taste it."

I paused for a moment as his words penetrated my lust-addled brain. That wasn't something I'd ever done before, or ever had the desire to do, if I was being honest. But as he stared down at me, one cocky brow arching like he was daring me not to follow direction, I felt something unlock inside of me. I remembered how he'd gone down on me that night like he couldn't get enough, the sounds he made and how he lapped at me like I was the most delicious thing he'd ever tasted. And suddenly I was eager to experience what he had.

Bringing my hand to my mouth, I sucked my finger between my lips, my eyes falling closed as my essence burst on my tongue. It wasn't good or bad, it was just . . . different. A step outside of my comfort zone, and that alone was a huge turn-on.

"That's it, baby. See why I loved the taste of that cunt so damn much? Tastes like heaven. My mouth has been watering for more for weeks."

I pulled the finger from my mouth with a pop and spread my legs even wider. My lips curled up in a lazy grin as my eyelids grew heavier. I wasn't sure when the punishment was supposed to start, but so far I was having a damn good time. "Then have another taste," I coaxed, barely recognizing my own voice. It was deep and throaty, dripping with lust and desire.

His grin was downright wicked as his hands moved to the waistband of his jeans. He worked the end of his black leather belt through the buckle and whipped the length through the loops of his jeans.

"Oh, baby. I plan on it."

He made quick work of removing the rest of his clothes, and once he stood before me completely naked, all those sexy tattoos and tantalizing muscles on display, my heart started beating faster.

Anticipation thrummed in my veins as he climbed onto the bed, coming to hover over me. I reached up to drag my fingers through his hair. I'd never really thought I'd like long hair on a man before, but I was quickly discovering I liked absolutely everything having to do with Pope.

But before I could touch him, he pulled back, his strong thighs straddling my hips, his long, thick cock straining upward toward his bellybutton. "Did I say you could touch me, Lennon?"

My brows furrowed in confusion. "I—"

He cut me off. "I think it's time we started your punishment."

SEVENTEEN

POPE

THOSE PALE GREEN eyes of hers flashed, and I took a second, watching closely to see how she'd react, but there was no fear in her gaze, only scorching need. She really did want to be punished.

Fuck, but she was perfect for me.

She licked her lips, her gaze bouncing from my dick to my face and back again, like she would die if she didn't get her mouth on me. It was enough to make my cock weep, beads of pre-cum dripping off the tip and splattering onto her chest.

She pulled in a sharp gasp as she looked at it slipping down her silky skin toward the valley between her perfect tits.

"See what you do to me?" I hissed between clenched teeth, desperation making my balls ache. I couldn't remember a time in my life when I'd been so keyed up. If

I didn't find a way to calm down, I wasn't going to last more than a handful of minutes. If that.

Her gaze returned to mine, her pupils so wide they nearly swallowed up all the color. "Pope," she whispered, goosebumps spreading across her entire body.

"Fuckin' love my name on your lips like that. Now be a good girl and give me your wrists."

She lay back, her lithe body stretching long beneath me, and lifted her arms, presenting her wrists to me. I didn't hesitate, wrapping the length of my belt around them, tying them together and pushing them against the pillows at the head of the bed. I took in her delicate wrists wrapped in the worn leather and had to clench my jaw to keep from rushing this. I pulled in a calming breath and looked back to her face, raising my brows in silent question. *Are you okay this?* She read my look loud and clear, nodding as she swallowed audibly.

"Leave them there. No matter what, don't move them."

Her mouth opened and closed a few times, shock blanketing her features. "But . . . I want to touch you."

Hearing that made my chest swell, but it didn't lessen my resolve. I smiled arrogantly. "Well you can't have what you want. That's what a punishment is, baby."

A whine vibrated in her throat, causing me to laugh before I planted my hands in the bed on either side of her shoulders and slammed my lips down on hers. It took an act of strength I didn't know I possessed to keep from lowering myself on top of her and driving my cock into her wet heat, but I somehow managed to refrain, dragging my lips from her mouth, down her neck, and past her collarbone.

I stopped to suck one of her perfect pink nipples into my mouth, pulling hard on it before nipping the tip with my teeth.

The noises she made, the way her body writhed, spurred me on. I wasn't being gentle. I was going to leave marks behind. But she was getting off on it every bit as much as I was. I sensed movement as I shifted to her other breast and cast my eyes up just in time to see her lifting her arms off the pillows.

"Ah, ah, ah," I chided. "What did I tell you about those hands?"

She dropped them back with a heavy plop, her chest heaving as I continued to move lower. The smell of her arousal as I got closer to that sweet cunt was quickly driving me crazy, and once I reached the apex of her thighs, I dove in, my mouth watering for her.

She cried out loudly at the first swipe of my tongue across her slit, her back arching off the bed, but she kept her hands in place like a good girl.

"Fucking ambrosia," I groaned into her pussy, lapping at those lips and licking up every drop. "That's what you taste like, Lennon. Pure, sweet, unfiltered heaven." I dove back in, her arousal dripped from her like honey, and I couldn't get enough. I alternated between spearing my tongue into her cunt and sucking at her clit, tuned into the noises she was making and the way her body reacted.

"Oh god, Pope." Her voice was coated in sex. "It's so good." Her moans increased in frequency when I plunged one finger inside her, pumping it in and out before adding a second, then a third, stretching her tight sheath so she'd be able to fit around my cock later.

After I finished with her punishment, of course.

I curled my fingers, brushing the pads of them against her G-spot as I sucked hard on her clit.

"*Yes!*" she shouted, her walls gripping my fingers as she got closer. "Pope, I'm going to—" Her words were cut off by a strangled cry when I slipped my drenched digits out of her and pulled away from her clit.

I looked up the length of her delectable body, finding she'd lifted her head and her glazed eyes were fixed on me. "What are you doing? I was so close."

"You don't get to come," I said, finally getting to the whole point of this.

Her eyes rounded and her jaw dropped. "What?"

"You don't get to come. That's part of your punishment, baby. I'm going to feast on this pussy until I've had my fill—and I'll warn you now, I'm fuckin' starved, so it'll take a while for me to get full."

"B-but—"

"I'm going to keep my face buried in your cunt, licking and sucking and fucking you with my fingers over and over until you get so close you're begging for it. But I still won't let you come. Not until I'm good and ready."

"You can't . . ." Her words died when I petted her slit, caressing her with soft, teasing touches that would do nothing but drive her insane.

"Maybe then you'll understand what I've been going through since I woke up and found you'd snuck out."

On that, I dove back in. I ate her out until my face was covered in her wetness, pushing her to the edge of that cliff over and over just to yank her back at the very last second every time, keeping her on edge and never letting up.

She screamed, she cursed me, she begged for more, but every time I felt those telltale flutters, I backed away. It felt like an eternity had passed by the time I lifted my head, taking in every inch of her flushed skin. I'd worked her so hard a thin sheen of sweat covered her body, and my jaw was beginning to throb, but I could have stayed down there for hours.

"Please, Pope," she begged when I pushed up on my arms to see her face clearly. Her pupils were blown, the green having been completely swallowed up. She looked like she'd been drugged and sounded as desperate as a junky craving their next fix.

"Oh god, Pope. Please. *Please.* I can't take it anymore." Her voice cracked. That was when I knew I had her.

"You had enough of being punished?" I asked, my voice deep and craggy. She wasn't the only one hanging on by her fingernails. The grip I had on my control was slowly peeling away, one finger at a time.

"Yes, *please.* I can't take it. I need . . ."

I braced myself on one hand while I slid the other back between her thighs, pushing my fingers past her swollen lips and deep into her channel. "What do you need?" Her eyes were screwed shut, her head thrashed back and forth, the sound coming from her throat nearly a sob. "You need to come?" I asked as I dragged my fingers in and out at a tortuously slow pace. "Is that what you were going to say? That you need me to make you come?"

Lennon's eyelids flew open, the fire I saw in her gaze matching the one I felt burning in my chest. Something inside me flipped over in that moment as our gazes locked. It was as if there was a magnet in my chest, pulling us together. I'd been there to witness some of my guys finding the women meant for them. Hell, I'd seen it in my father every single day he looked at my mom before we lost her. But I never thought I'd experience it for myself.

But as Lennon's penetrating gaze drilled into me, it was like being hit with a bolt of lightning. This woman was it. She fit into all those jagged, twisting places inside of me like she'd been made just for me. She was created to be the queen I kept at my side.

"Pope, please," she whispered, "make me come. I need it."

She was right there, I could feel it in the way she was clenching my fingers like a vise. Ripping my hand away, I grabbed my cock, lined it up with her entrance and drove in hard. That was all it took. As soon as I bottomed out, every muscle in her body locked tight and that coil I'd been twisting inside her snapped. Her pussy clamped down around me as she threw her head back, and her spine arched off the mattress as she screamed with the release I'd been denying her for the past thirty minutes.

The effort to hold still as her pussy tried desperately to milk my cock was so painful my teeth clamped down on the inside of my cheek hard enough for me to taste blood.

"Oh god, oh shit, *Pope!*" Lennon shouted as her climax dragged on for what felt like an eternity before her body finally collapsed back onto the bed. She panted like she'd sprinted her way through an entire marathon as she peeled those sea foam eyes open and looked at me.

"Fuck," I grunted, still planted deep in her cunt. "Do you have any goddamn clue how sexy you look when you come?"

Her throat rasped on a whimper. "Move," she pleaded, circling her hips beneath me.

I couldn't stop the smirk from curling my lips upward. "You need me to fuck you, baby?"

"So bad. Please."

The feel of her was like nothing I'd ever experienced before. Then the realization of why slammed into me. *"Fuckin' hell,"* I hissed, grinding my molars together as I grabbed hold of her hip to stop her from moving. "No condom." Christ, this woman did something to my head. I'd never gone ungloved in all the years I'd been having sex. Not even if the woman assured me she was covered. It was one of those rules I never broke—those very same rules I'd blown straight to hell the night I met Lennon.

Her eyes widened for just a second before lowering to half-mast as she pulled her bottom lip between her teeth. I'd pull out if that was what she wanted. I'd force myself to slip out of heaven so I could slide on a rubber if she said I needed to, but I silently pleaded with every higher power I'd ever heard of to make her say yes, because being bare inside her was the most incredible thing I'd ever felt.

"I'm clean," I assured her, hoping that would sway her decision. "I've never once gone bare. Not ever."

"I-I'm clean too," she said quietly. "I got tested after—"

I slammed my mouth down on hers, cutting her off because I knew exactly what she was going to say, and I didn't want her to have to force the rest of the words out. She'd gotten tested after finding out that fuckhead ex-husband of hers had cheated.

"You protected?" I asked when I finally ended the slow, languid kiss.

She nodded, her cheeks flushed. "IUD."

Thank fuck. "Does that mean I can have you bare, Lennon? 'Cause I think I might have a goddamn heart attack if I don't fuck you."

Her lips winged up in a smile that slammed into my chest like a wrecking ball. "Yes, you can fuck me bare. But I have a request." I arched a brow and waited for her to lay it on me. And what she asked for lit me up from the inside out. "Will you grab my throat again? Like you did earlier?"

Fucking perfect for me.

I answered by letting out a feral growl and reaching up to collar her delicate throat as I pulled out and slammed back in hard enough to make her cry out.

"You mean like this, Raven?" I drove my cock into her again and again, clenching my fingers around her throat just hard enough to feel the frantic beat of her pulse beneath her skin. "You want to be fucked like this? Raw and dirty?"

"Yes," she hissed. "Don't be gentle. Make me feel it for days."

There was something behind her request, a deeper meaning, but that was a conversation for another time. What little control I had left disappeared in a puff of smoke. There was a beast inside me that came to life, and I let it loose as I fucked this perfect woman like she was made only for me. I drove into her, over and over, each punishing thrust hard enough that the headboard slammed against the wall.

"Oh *fuck!*" she shouted, her eyes going wide as her pussy began to pulse around me with another impending orgasm. "*Yes*, Pope. Just like that. Please don't stop."

"Never," I gritted out, curling my lips away from my teeth as my balls drew up close to my body and the base of my spine started to tingle. I pushed back on my haunches, grabbing her by the waist and yanking her up so her ass was resting on my lap and her thighs were spread wide over mine. From that vantage point I could see my cock driving in and out of her cunt, glistening with her arousal as it soaked me. I could watch those perfect tits bounce as I fucked her with abandon. I could take in my tattooed hand wrapped around her throat and those bound wrists still draped over her head.

Having her like that was a fucking voyeur's delight. Every inch a turn-on.

"Yes, Pope. Yes. Just like that." Her moans came faster as the head of my cock dragged against her G-spot while I powered in and out of her. I kept that hand at her throat but moved the other to where we were connected, pressing my thumb to her clit and circling as the release building in my balls threatened to overtake me. My movement became erratic as I held back as long as I possibly could. Then her cunt closed around my cock like a fist and Lennon went off again, dragging me along with her that time.

Throwing my head back, I let out a guttural shout that turned into a feral growl as I came, my release shooting deep inside her. Her pussy milked me, each pulse of her climax squeezing more from my cock until there was absolutely nothing left.

"Holy fuck," she breathed, her voice sounding like it was coming from inside a fishbowl as I blinked my eyes, trying to bring everything back into focus.

Jesus, I'd never come like that before, so fucking hard and long I thought the back of my skull was about to blow off.

Every inch of her delectable little body was glowing with a pink flush, our skin misted with sweat from the workout we'd just put in. Finally, I peeled my fingers back from her throat, my eyes on her fuck-drunk expression. "You okay?" I asked, the words dragging up my parched throat like sandpaper. That had been the best fuck of my entire life, but now that the haze of lust had cleared, I couldn't help but worry I'd been too rough.

However, the brilliant smile she hit me with was enough to ease all my concerns. "I'm *amazing*."

A chuckle rattled my chest. She certainly fucking was. I slid my hands down her ribs and the feminine dip of her waist before coming to rest on her hips, my eyes zeroing in on where we were still connected. I shifted my hips back, allowing my semi-hard dick to slip free, and at the sight of my cum spilling out of her, something primal roared to life deep inside me. I'd marked her skin with my mouth before, but this was different. As my essence, mingled with hers, dripped from her, it took everything I had to keep from pounding my chest as my cock thickened once more.

Gripping my shaft in my hand, I gathered up what had slid from her pussy with the head of my cock and slowly fed my length back into her.

Her eyes widened, her lips parting on a gasp as I forced my cum back inside her. "Again? *Already*?" she asked in bewilderment, earning a cocky smirk from me.

"Oh, Raven. I'm just getting started."

EIGHTEEN

LENNON

THE WIND WHIPPING over my face and lifting my hair was a sensation I wasn't used to. I'd only been on a motorcycle one other time, the night I'd met Pope, but I'd been so focused on him and what was to come after fooling around on the hood of that car, I hadn't been able to really appreciate the ride. That desperation was still there, bubbling beneath the surface, but after so many orgasms I'd nearly lost count, I was sated enough to actually enjoy the experience for the first time.

Not to say I wasn't also a jumble of nerves for other reasons. After all, between the punishment that had almost been enough to literally drive me crazy and him sinking deep inside me, something major had happened. There had been a shift. I couldn't put a name to it—or maybe I was too scared to try—but I did know whatever had happened, it was profound enough to knock my world right off its axis.

He'd fucked me twice more before I finally declared that I needed a break, and after returning from my bathroom with a damp washcloth and taking it upon himself to clean me up—something no other man had ever done for me—he'd announced that I needed to get dressed so he could feed me.

It was late. I was tired and didn't have a clue if anything was still open, but I also wasn't quite ready to say goodbye to him. So I donned a pair of leggings and a cozy sweater, and climbed on the back of his bike.

I didn't miss Otto and Esther's porch light flipping on just seconds after the rumble of Pope's bike started up, the sound filling the night air, or the door opening and the couple stepping out as Pope used his feet to back us out of the driveway. But when I lifted an arm from around his waist and waved in their direction before we zipped down my street, I caught Ether's shameless smile and knew whatever had gone down earlier was firmly behind us. At least for her. Otto still looked worried, but Esther looked ecstatic.

I tipped my head back, smiling at the stars that dotted the sky. That was another one of the things I loved so much about Ashland, something I'd never gotten in the city. I'd never seen so many stars in my life. The black sky was covered in millions of tiny white specks. And for some reason the view from the back of Pope's bike made it even more spectacular.

My focus shifted away from the sky and back on the man I was currently clinging to when I felt the motorcycle decelerate. I glanced around at the houses lining either side of the street. I'd expected to head into the heart of town where most of the bars and restaurants were, not into a residential neighborhood—a neighborhood that was starting to look awfully familiar.

"Where are we going?" I called over the thunderous sound of the engine.

He released one of the handlebars after coming to a stop at a stop sign, his hand landing on my forearm wrapped around his abdomen and giving it a squeeze as he looked back over his shoulder. "Told you, I'm feeding you."

With that, he took off once more, and I held on as he wound his way from street to street before finally pulling up in front of his house a few short minutes later.

He parked in front of the house I'd all but run from that morning that felt like an eternity ago and killed the engine before reaching back to give my thigh a squeeze. "Hop off, baby."

I scrambled off the back of the bike and wobbled a bit as residual vibrations from the engine crawled up my legs. There was no missing the appeal of riding a motor-cycle, but it would clearly take some getting used to. I unclipped the helmet he'd plopped on my head back at my place and handed it to him before looking up at his house. A few strategically placed lights had been left on inside, casting a warm, golden glow through the large windows that made up most of the front of his house.

Thanks to the wild night before and the huge hang-over that came the morning after, I'd convinced myself I had imagined how beautiful Pope's home was, but as I looked up at it, I realized it hadn't been my imagination at all. His home was stunning. But I still didn't under-stand why we were there.

"I thought you said you were going to feed me." As if my stomach understood what I was saying, it chose that moment to let out a *loud* gurgle, announcing it was way past time to eat.

Pope chuckled as my cheeks heated. "I am." He took my hand and led me up the walkway and porch steps to the front door.

"Then why are we here instead of a restaurant? Or the diner. You know, I heard they have pretty good pie there."

"The pie at Al's is the best in the state. I'll take you there some other time. But tonight, I'm cookin' for you."

At that declaration, I nearly tripped over my own feet, my mouth falling open in shock.

He punched a few buttons on a keypad attached to the door, and it let out a short mechanical chime followed by the sound of the deadbolt turning. Pushing the door open, he reached inside and flipped on a light switch that illuminated the whole entryway and stepped aside, lifting an arm to wave me in. His house smelled like him, like leather and spice mixed with a hint of cedar. It was masculine and intoxicating. I wanted to bottle the scent and spray it all over my pillows so I could go to sleep every night to his smell.

He tossed his keys on a console table that held a few pieces of mail, some loose change, and whatever else he pulled from his pockets. The leather vest I'd been up close and personal with on the ride here was stripped off and hung on a hook by the door with care, next to a leather jacket that had the same insignia.

I suddenly recalled everything Iris had told me about Pope and his club. A million questions zipped through my mind about that patch and what it meant, but before I could find the words to ask them, he took my hand and led me deeper into the house. The kitchen was at the back and much larger than I had expected. It was even bigger than the kitchen in the house I'd shared with Oliver, with top-of-the-line appliances and sleek, pale counters that complimented the midnight blue of the cabinets.

The kitchen was any cook's dream, and while I was

impressed by it, it sure as hell didn't give me any sort of niggling to get back in there and whip up a meal.

Fortunately, it seemed Pope didn't expect me to help with anything, because as soon as we rounded the counter and stepped into the space, he pulled out one of the stools tucked against the island. "Make yourself comfortable. You can keep me company while I cook. You want something to drink?" he asked as he moved to the stainless-steel fridge and pulled the door open. "Don't have much. There's soda, beer, and water." He looked back at me over his shoulder. "I've got a bottle of whiskey in the cabinet if you're in the mood for somethin' stronger." He shot me a wink as his lips tipped up in a knowing smirk. "Or maybe some tequila?"

I gave him a smile, shaking my head on a quiet giggle. "Water, please. Thank you."

He moved to one of the cabinets and opened it, removing a glass and filling it from the spout on the front of the fridge. He placed it on the island in front of me before reaching up and circling my neck with his large hand and using his thumb to tilt my chin upward. The kiss he planted on my lips was more claiming than it was sweet, and managed to heat my blood as it rushed through my veins.

I watched in a bit of a daze as he moved around his kitchen with ease, pulling ingredients from the fridge and pantry and lining them along the island across from me. "Any allergies I should know about? Or anything you don't like to eat?"

I shook my head as warmth bloomed in my chest. I had to clear my throat against the lump that had suddenly formed there. "Uh, no. I'm not really picky. If you make it, I'll eat it," I answered truthfully, but apparently the look on my face gave me away.

"Hey," Pope said in such a gentle tone I was a little taken aback. I had no clue the massive, rugged, dirty-talking man was capable of such softness. I would have been lying if I said I didn't love the contrast between his hard and his soft. "Talk to me, Raven. What's goin' through that head of yours right now?"

I sniffled, not realizing just how emotional I'd gotten at this man asking such a simple question. I waved him off, trying my best to play it cool. "It's nothing. Really. I'm just being silly."

He rounded the island, coming back over to me, and took my chin between his fingers, forcing me to meet his gaze. "If it has to do with you, I want to know. Not sure you've gotten it by now, baby, but I want to know everything about you."

God. This man. He made it damn near impossible to maintain any sort of distance.

"It's just . . ." My mind spun, trying to find the words that wouldn't make me sound ridiculous. "You asked if there was anything I didn't like," I said like that made any sense, and I could see by the furrow of his brow he was more confused than ever, so I pushed on, trying to explain. "You're cooking for me, and I've never had a person cook for me before."

His brows winged up toward his hairline. "Never? What about your parents?"

I shook my head, the smile on my face small and sad. "Not that I have any recollection of. My mom passed when I was really little, and my dad . . . well, he didn't really have a lot of time for me." God, I hated admitting that—no matter how true it was. "I had to start taking care of myself at a really young age, and eventually I taught myself to cook so I could feed me and my dad. Then Oliver always wanted a homecooked meal, and, well . . ." I trailed off, lifting my shoulder in a shrug. "He never cared much for what I liked or didn't like. If he wanted it, he expected me to cook it."

"So now you hate cooking."

I nodded, appreciating that he understood. "Now I hate cooking."

Pope trailed his hand around to the back of my neck, squeezing the muscles there and pulling a faint moan from me as he worked the knots loose. "Your ex is a fuckin' moron, baby. I hope you know that. But it doesn't matter anymore, because I'm more than capable of finding my way around the kitchen."

To prove his point, he released me and got to work. I

sat on the stool with my legs crossed, one elbow resting on the counter, and my chin propped in my palm as I watched him make dinner. And it wasn't some simple boil and eat dish either. He made shrimp alfredo, with pasta noodles he made *from scratch*. He even had one of those pasta attachment thingies to go on the KitchenAid mixer he pulled out of the pantry. That's right, he owned a *KitchenAid mixer*.

I wasn't sure I'd ever witnessed anything sexier than this big tattooed man kneading and working a ball of pasta dough. It was the ultimate food porn. Not only were his skills impressive, but the meal itself was incredible. The man didn't only know his way around a kitchen, he freaking dominated it, blowing anything I could have cooked right out of the water.

Then, as if he couldn't possibly get any better, when I tried rinsing the dishes and cleaning up after him, he'd handed me one of the beers in his fridge and shooed me out of the kitchen, telling me to head out to the deck and he'd meet me there when he finished.

I opened the sliding glass door off the kitchen and stepped into the chilled night, closing my eyes and pulling in a deep breath as I centered myself.

It wasn't the incredible sex that was going to do me it. Or at least not *just* the incredible sex. It was the gentle touches and soft looks. It was the fact that he wanted to cook for me and didn't expect anything in return for doing it. It was the way he could fuck me hard and dirty one moment, then be sweet and tender the next.

There was still so much I didn't know about this man, but the more time I spent with him, the less I cared about anything else.

And that was what made him so damn dangerous.

NINETEEN

LENNON

I SAT in the middle of The Daily Grind, sipping my latte as I waited for Iris to process everything I'd just told her. It was late Sunday morning, and after spending most of the weekend with Pope, having more sex in those couple days than I had in the entire six months prior, I'd finally come up for air long enough to meet Iris and Phoebe for brunch.

Phoebe ate her muffin slowly, watching Iris with concern. "Is she okay?" she asked, pointing at Iris. "She hasn't blinked for at least a minute. Is that normal? Her eyes have to be super dry, right?"

"I think she's okay." At least I hoped so. I didn't have many friends, so I would hate to have broken one already.

Iris finally showed signs of life by shaking herself out of her stupor. "I'm sorry. So, this guy gives multiple orgasms out like candy, he cooks for you, *and* he looks like he belongs on the set of *Vikings* as a freaking stunt double?" Her bewildered expression morphed into a glare. "You know I kind of hate you right now, right?"

I hid my grin behind the lid of my coffee cup.

"I'm serious," she exclaimed on a pout. "I haven't had sex in so long I'm embarrassed to admit it, and even then, a hard sneeze would have felt better than what that guy did in bed."

The sip I'd just taken went down the wrong way, and I proceeded to choke as Phoebe cackled loud enough to draw attention.

"You laugh, but I'm not joking," Iris continued. "He rutted around in there like a truffle pig digging for mushrooms. And when he came he shouted 'and boom goes the dynamite'. Uh, hate to break it to you my guy, but there was definitely no boom on my end." She shook her head in disgust. "Disappointing as hell."

"Oh my God," I giggled uncontrollably. "You have to stop. There's a mom right over there pushing a stroller."

She flopped back in her chair, crossing her arms over her chest indignantly. "This is so not fair. You're married"—she pointed to Phoebe then me—"and you're getting the goods from Jax Teller 4.0. When's it going to be Iris's turn, huh?"

I was pretty sure Pope wouldn't be thrilled with being compared to a TV character, but what he didn't know wouldn't hurt him. And I had to admit, it was a pretty apt description.

"Hey, you're going to find someone," I insisted, reaching across the table and placing my hand on top of hers. It was what I truly believed, because I couldn't for the life of me imagine that the men in this town wouldn't see Iris for the incredible woman she was. It was only a matter of time. "And it's not like Pope and I are this major thing. I mean, it was just a weekend." A really amazing, life-altering weekend. "It's not like we're a serious couple. We're just . . . having fun. I mean, we still barely know each other."

She pinched her lips to the side and gave me a flat look, as if to say, *Seriously? Who do you think you're fooling?*

Phoebe didn't appear to be buying it either. "Tell me, what did he say when he dropped you off at your place this morning?"

I turned my focus on her. "He said to have fun and he'd call me."

"Was it just a blanket 'I'll call you' or was he specific?" Iris asked.

I lifted my shoulder in a shrug. "What's it matter?"

"Context always matters," Phoebe stated seriously.

I thought back to earlier that morning when Pope had dropped me off at my house. I'd spent two incredible nights in his bed and as much as I wanted to stay curled up in the little bubble we'd managed to create, I knew it was time for me to get back to the real world. He'd tried to talk me into coming back to his house once I finished brunch, but I'd begged off, telling him I really needed to do laundry and I had papers to grade. As much fun as I'd had with him, I felt like maybe a little space would help me get my head out of the clouds and my feet back on the ground. I really liked him, but I was still terrified I'd lose myself in another man.

After another ride on his bike, he'd walked me to the door, giving Otto and Esther a friendly wave and laying a scorching kiss on me that made my knees wobbly. Then he'd tucked my hair behind my ear with that soft look on his face and told me he'd call me later that night and couldn't wait to see me again.

"He said he'd call tonight."

Phoebe arched a brow, staring me down like she knew I was holding something back. "*And.*"

I took a big gulp of my latte. "And . . . he might have said he wasn't looking forward to going to sleep without me beside him tonight," I admitted on a mumble.

Iris threw her hands in the air. "There you go. It's more serious than you're willing to admit."

Phoebe nodded in agreement. "She's right babe. Sounds to me like that guy is all in. Mike acted the same way after our first full weekend together, and look at me now." She held her arms out at her sides. "Two kids who could quite possibly be the future destroyers of the world and married fifteen years to a man who has some sort of radar that alerts him every time I bend over so he can come up behind and hump me." Her tone might have made it seem like she was annoyed, but the smile she was desperately trying to fight back told me she was actually really happy with her lot in life, and I loved that for her.

I dropped my face into my hands and let out a groan. "This wasn't supposed to happen. I *just* got divorced. The last thing I should do is step into something serious. I mean, don't you think it's too soon?"

Iris shot me a wry smile and looked to Phoebe. "She planned and the big man upstairs laughed."

"Or big woman," she corrected, lifting her finger in the air. "And yep. Because that's usually how it goes." Turning to me, she said, "Honey, these things tend to happen whether you're prepared for them or not. Your ex was a massive bag of dicks—"

"A cockwaffle!" Iris interrupted loudly, extremely proud of her new insult for Oliver.

Phoebe nodded in approval. "Ooh, I like it. He was a real cockwaffle. But you can't let one bad experience taint all future relationships for you."

My throat felt dry all of a sudden, and I had trouble swallowing the drink of coffee I'd just taken. "But . . ." I cast a furtive glance around the coffee shop to make sure no one was listening before leaning in and lowering my voice. "But what about the whole motorcycle club thing?" I looked to Iris. "You said it yourself, there are rumors. What if—what if he's not a good guy?"

The moment that question passed my lips, my stomach revolted, twisting into knots. The voice in the back of my head cursed me for making a snap judgment. Everything in my body screamed that I knew better, that Pope had proven himself to be a good guy simply by how he'd treated me. Sure the red flags were there, but deep down, I knew he was a good man.

And I could tell by the expression on my friends' faces they knew it too.

"You don't really believe that, do you?" Iris asked me, her tone indicating she already knew the answer.

My shoulders slumped and I lowered my head as shame coursed through me. "No. I don't really believe that."

Phoebe braced her forearms on the table and leaned in. "Look, I know there are stories floating all around, and maybe there's truth to some of them. But I also know that last year, when the district was talking about laying off teachers because there wasn't enough money in the budget, that club donated a huge chunk of cash so no one had to lose their job." My heart skipped a few beats at that information.

Iris chimed in, adding another tally mark in Pope's

favor. "And their garage always sponsors one of the pee-wee football teams."

Phoebe's hand landed on top of mine, giving it a squeeze. "You can't punish one man for the sins of another. If you have questions, *talk to him*. But don't paint him with your ex-cockwaffle's brush unless you're certain he deserves it."

As I sat on my loveseat later that evening, the test papers I was grading spread out around me, I couldn't stop thinking about what Phoebe had said. It was taking up so much space in my brain that I was having trouble concentrating on the work I was supposed to be doing.

She was right. I was holding Pope accountable for all the shit Oliver and my father had put me through because I was scared of getting hurt again. But that wasn't fair to him.

Finally giving up on the paper I was supposed to be reading, I slapped it down on the cushion beside me and snatched up my phone, scrolling to my text messages. However, before I could figure out what to type, the screen lit up and the phone rang.

At the sight of Pope's name flashing across the screen,

a smile big enough to make my cheeks hurt stretched across my face. The first ring had barely ended when I swiped my thumb across the glass to answer and lifted it to my ear. "Hey," I said softly, my chest feeling warm and fuzzy. "I was just thinking about you."

His rich, husky chuckle carried through the line, sending sparks through my blood. "Love hearing that, darlin'. But do me a favor and come open the door, would you? My hands are full."

"You're here?" Excitement burst through me as I jumped off the loveseat and rushed to the front door. I yanked it open just as his booted foot hit my bottom porch step. His smile hit me center-mass and spread through my entire body until it felt like bursts of light were shooting from the tips of my fingers and toes. "Hi," I said on a whisper, frozen inside the doorway as he closed the distance between us.

"Hey, baby," he said in that gentle way of his that was *really* growing on me. He lifted the Chinese takeout bag he carried in one hand and the grocery bag in the other. "I know you're busy, but I couldn't stand the thought of you livin' off any of that shit you have in the freezer, so I figured I'd bring you some dinner. I can drop it and go if you need to get back to work."

This man.

I reached out, fisting the fabric of his T-shirt beneath his leather vest and yanked him to me as I lifted up on my toes and pressed my lips to his. "Or you could stay and eat with me." Then I decided the hell with it. I liked this man, and I was done being scared. "I missed you."

His grin turned into a full-blown smile at my confession, and he leaned down for another kiss, this one hard and claiming. "Missed you too, baby. And I'll stay as long as you want."

I led him inside, heading for the cabinet that held the stash of paper plates I'd picked up at the store while he unloaded the bags.

"Wasn't sure what you liked, so I got a variety," he stated as he pulled Chinese food containers out and set them on the island. It smelled like heaven. From the grocery bag he pulled out a six-pack of the beer he favored, along with two bottles of the red wine I preferred.

My eyes bugged out as I lifted them to him. "How did you know that's the wine I like?"

He shrugged like it was nothing as he pulled open drawers in search of silverware. Luckily I had that, along with a few glasses so we didn't have to drink out of plastic cups. "Saw you had a bottle of it open on the counter last time I was here, so I just assumed."

On that declaration, something deep inside my chest snapped back into place. It was a piece broken off by my father then stomped on by Oliver. A piece I'd been convinced was beyond repair. But in a handful of days, this incredible man had somehow managed to fix it and glue it right back where it belonged.

I swallowed the ball of emotion that had formed in my throat and pulled my bottom lip between my teeth as I looked up at Pope through the fan of my lashes. "You know what's even better than hot Chinese food?"

His gaze came to me. "What's that, baby?"

I grinned wickedly, silently communicating exactly what I was feeling. "Cold Chinese food."

With that, I turned and darted out of the kitchen on a laugh. A second later, the sound of Pope's boots thudded against the floor as he chased after me.

TWENTY

LENNON

I LAY STRETCHED out across Pope's chest, feeling more content than I had in a very long time, as he traced random patterns on my naked back and hip with his fingertips.

"Thank you," I said into the quiet of the room.

"For what, Raven?"

For everything, I thought, but I made my answer more specific. "For dinner. And for the wine. For paying attention and actually caring. That's not something I'm used to."

He shifted under me, wrapping an arm around my waist to hold me to him as he pushed himself up to sitting. He rested his back against the headboard as I straddled his waist, my breasts pressed against his hard, defined pecs. Those midnight eyes burrowed into me as he reached up to brush a lock of hair away from my fore-head and tuck it behind my ear.

"I haven't asked about your fucker of an ex because I didn't want to cast a shadow over what we have happening here. But I think maybe it's time."

He wasn't wrong, but that didn't mean I was looking forward to the conversation.

"Cockwaffle," I said out of nowhere.

His chin tucked back into his neck in confusion. "What?"

"Cockwaffle. That's the name my friend Iris came up with to describe my ex. He's a cockwaffle."

Pope's body shook with quiet laughter, the rumble in his chest seeping into mine and warming me from the inside out. "You can call him whatever you want, baby. But you gotta know, I'm not gonna use that word."

I lifted my shoulders in a shrug. "Your loss. Cock-waffle is a brilliant word."

"If you say so," he said with a brilliant grin. "Look, Raven, we don't have to talk about this if you don't want to. I thought that it might help you feel better to get it all off your chest. That, and knowing will help me navigate what we have going here. The more I know, the better I can avoid any landmines so I don't do something that could hurt you."

Gah!

Of course he wasn't asking because he was curious or

nosey. He was asking because he wanted to be better equipped to take care of *me*. No one had ever done that, and if he didn't stop being so damn sweet, I was liable to burst into tears.

"No, I want you to know." I traced his strong, square jaw, shivering at the delicious rasp of the blond stubble abrading my skin. I was very familiar with that stubble, and I particularly enjoyed how it felt between my thighs. "Besides, you said you wanted to know everything about me, right?"

"Absolutely. But only what you're comfortable sharing."

In that moment, I knew. I wanted to share it all with this man. So that was exactly what I did. I started from the beginning, telling him about my childhood and my father who hadn't cared one way or another if I was around unless it was time for me to handle something around the house so he didn't have to. I told him about feeling lonely for so damn long that when Oliver came around, I'd slipped on rose-colored glasses so I wouldn't have to see the warning signs. I confessed that my marriage had been lousy, and I'd played a part because I sat back and let him get away with whatever he wanted because I didn't want to rock the boat. I told him all about the cheating and the bullshit excuses he gave me about sleeping with those other women because he wanted to keep what we had pure.

I wasn't sure what I expected him to say once I finally got the whole ugly story out, but he left me speechless when he gently lifted me off his lap, depositing me on the mattress, and climbed out of the bed, donning his boxer briefs before walking out of the room.

I stared after him, flabbergasted, trying to figure out what the actual hell had just happened, when he reappeared a minute later with a glass of wine filled all the way to the top and a beer.

He passed me the glass and climbed back into bed before opening the beer and sucking down half.

"Uh . . ."

"Figured you'd need a fuckin' drink after sharing all that shit. And Christ knows I do after hearing how every man in your life has basically let you down when they should have been lookin' out for you."

I took a couple massive gulps of wine, hoping it would keep me from turning into a blubbering mess. "Okay, you've got to stop being so perfect, or I'm going to lose it. I don't know if it makes me want to cry or have sex again, but if you don't knock it off, there's a good chance it'll end up being both, and I don't think either of us would enjoy me sobbing all over you while you're inside me."

Pope chuckled, setting his beer down on the one nightstand I bought when I got the bed, and took my half-drunk glass of wine and did the same. He reached over and grabbed me, bringing me back to his lap so he could run his palms up and down my waist. "Pretty sure I'd enjoy fucking you no matter what, but you need to know, I'm not perfect, Raven."

There was something in his gaze that made it hard for me to pull in a full breath, something like shame and sadness, like he was carrying a weight on his shoulders all by himself, and seeing as he'd been there for me, I felt it was only right to return the favor.

"Hey," I said softly, sliding my fingers into his hair at his temples and tilting his face up to mine. "Talk to me. What's going on in that head of yours?"

His chest expanded on a deep inhale. "I wasn't lookin' for someone like you. I thought I was fine with the way my life was going, then you came out of left field, baby. What I feel for you is not somethin' I've ever experienced before, and even though I don't want to lose you, you need to know the truth. I'm not a good man, Lennon. There's shit in my past that would scare you. Some of it I regret, but some of it I don't, because I did what I did to protect the people I care about, and I'd be lyin' if I said I wouldn't do it again if it meant keepin' them safe."

My heart started beating faster. Given my past, my first instinct was to run, but I shoved that feeling away and stayed where I was, giving him the chance to get it all out.

"Is this about your club?"

He squeezed his eyes closed and dropped his head back against the headboard, breathing slowly like he was counting to ten.

"Small town gossip can be a fuckin' bitch. Guess I shouldn't be surprised you've heard things."

"I have. But you should know, not all of them were bad. In fact, I heard a whole lot of good things, too."

His palms settled on my hips and his fingers clenched tight, pressing deep into my skin. "And that's what I spent years bustin' my ass to get us to. I wanted to take my club legit because I saw the damage that could be done with the shit we were doin'. People got hurt. Some of my men lost people they cared about. We did fucked-up shit, and we got paid to do it. But I saw the road our choices were leading us down, and I didn't like that. The Wraiths mean everything to me. They're the family I chose. I can't pretend we don't have a shady past, but what you need to know is we're out of all that now."

I continued with my soothing touch, hoping the gentle caress would put him at ease. "I can't imagine how hard that must have been, pulling your friends out of the bad and trying to lead them to something good like that," I said, my expression softening when he looked up at me in surprise. "Did you lose a lot of members?"

I could see the sadness reflecting in his eyes at my

question. He had. And I was sure at least a few of them had meant a lot to him. "My old man had already passed by the time I put my plan into motion. Lost some of the older guys because they didn't feel like followin' someone younger. Times were changing, and they struggled with those changes. Then there were those who didn't want to give up the money we were pullin' in or the adrenaline rush that came with the shit we were mixed up with. Some guys moved, others joined rival clubs. That last one was a serious fuckin' blow. It's one thing to lose family, but it's different when they choose to betray you."

"I'm so sorry."

He pulled me closer, leaning down enough to press a kiss right between my breasts. "We had some trouble with a former member not too long ago, a brother we had to kick out. He didn't take to goin' straight like the rest of us, and honestly, I wasn't surprised. There'd always been somethin' wrong with him. But he stole from the club to set up a little drug venture for himself behind our backs. Started causing problems one town over in Redemption, so me and my men had to handle it. But we haven't had an issue like that in a long time. For the most part, we're just a bunch of mechanics who like to drink and have a good time."

I didn't know what he meant by *handle it*, and honestly, I didn't want to. The man had a checkered past, there wasn't any doubt about it, but he knew what was right, and he'd gone through the wringer trying to lead his friends—his *family*—in that direction. I wasn't going to pretend to understand the ins and outs of the world he'd been raised in. But I knew a good man when I saw one, and Pope was a good man.

"I think you're being too hard on yourself."

He heaved out a sigh and started to shake his head, but I fisted my hands in those long, silky strands to hold him in place, making his nostrils flair and his gaze flash with heat.

"Yes, you've done some things I'm probably better off not knowing about, but I also know that you're the kind of man who'd make another man pay for putting his hands on his girlfriend." At the surprise filtering through his expression I arched a brow as if to say *uh huh, I heard about that, buddy*. I also know you and your men don't sit back and watch shit happen. You step in, whether that means donating money to a school or sponsoring a bunch of little boys who want to play football. A bad man wouldn't do things like that."

"Lennon—"

"I saw you with your niece," I said, cutting him off. "But more importantly, I saw her with you. I saw the way her entire being lit up at the sight of you because of the love she has for you. A bad man wouldn't garner that kind of loyalty and admiration. Men living a certain way-of-life wouldn't decide to throw it all away and push through the hard times alongside their friend if he wasn't a man worth following." I held his cheeks in my palms and leaned in close, pressing my forehead to his. "I've known bad men. I've known cowards and self-centered assholes. And I know You. Are. Not. That. A bad man wouldn't care about anyone but himself. So cut yourself some slack, baby. Because you're a good man."

The growl he let out as he fisted his hands in my hair and gripped it tight was so damn sexy it sent a flood of arousal to my core.

"Christ, you're really somethin', you know that? That motherfucker's loss is my gain."

I let out a shuddered breath as my nipples stiffened into tight peaks. I couldn't get enough of this man. It was so bad I was starting to think I was addicted, but I didn't have it in me to care.

"That Chinese food's sat for a long time already. What's another thirty minutes?" I teased, lifting my shoulder in a shrug as I reached between us and wrapped my fist around Pope's straining cock.

"Oh, Raven, this is gonna take a hell of a lot longer than that." He swatted my ass, giving it a stinging slap and eliciting a gasp from me. "Now get on your hands and knees so I can fuck you like the dirty girl you are."

I didn't have to be told twice.

TWENTY-ONE

LENNON

THE BELL RANG, signaling the end of class, so I hurried to stand as the kids started filtering out into the hall, hoping to catch Marigold before she had a chance to disappear.

It had been a week and a half since I'd stopped trying to fight my feelings for Pope, and for the most part, it had turned out to be some of the best days of my life. There was just one little problem that kept it from being nothing but sunshine and rainbows.

"Marigold, would you mind staying back for a second?"

She paused before exiting the classroom, pulling her bottom lip between her teeth as she turned away from her friends and looked back at me. I could see the curiosity on the faces of the girls she always hung out with, so I made sure to pin a smile to my face. "It'll only take a moment."

"Yeah, okay." She looked back at her friends. "I'll catch up with you guys at lunch."

I waited for the last student to leave and shut the door before looking back at the girl I'd watched closely all week long, and there wasn't a doubt in my mind that something was off. Her hair hung flat and limp around her shoulders like she'd gone a day longer than she should have between washes. The normal glow in her cheeks was gone, her complexion looking paler than usual, and she walked with her shoulders hunched, like she was trying to curl in on herself.

"Am I in trouble?" she asked, pulling me from my perusal. Even her voice was smaller than usual. She looked tired . . . and sad.

"No, of course not." I felt my features soften as I gave her a genuine smile. "Don't tell the other kids, but you're one of my best students," I teased, hoping to get some sort of reaction out of her, but she remained as stoic as ever. "I'm just concerned about you is all. You haven't seemed like yourself this week. Is everything all right?"

She curled her lips upward in a sad impression of a smile that didn't come anywhere near her eyes. "Yeah, everything's fine."

My heart squeezed. "Are you sure? You know, if

something's happening, you can always talk to me. I'm here for you any time."

"Everything's good, Ms. Cody. I just haven't felt great is all. I think it's a cold or something. I'll get over it."

"Okay. If you say so," I said, the skepticism in my voice ringing loud and clear.

"I promise. I'm good." She threw her thumb over her shoulder and started backing away. "I gotta get to Algebra. See you tomorrow."

"See you then."

My next class started filtering in, the students taking their seats, so I hurried to my desk and pulled out my phone, shooting off a quick text to Phoebe and a few more of my teacher friends, asking them to keep an eye on Marigold. I'd give her a few more days, but I'd watch closely, and if things didn't change, I was going to Pope with my concerns, whether she liked it or not.

Phoebe had asked if I wanted to grab a drink with her at Toni's Tavern after work, but by the time my last class ended, I was dead on my feet. All I could think about doing was soaking my sore feet and back in a nice, hot bath while I waited for Pope to head over to my place with dinner.

He was picking up food from a place he swore made the best burgers I'd ever eat, and I was looking forward to stuffing my face before passing out on my tiny couch, snuggled up with him while he caught up on a few episodes of some cop show he'd been watching on Netflix.

I turned onto my street, silently counting down the seconds until I could slip into my bath, when I spotted a shiny black sedan parked in my spot in my driveway.

"What now," I grumbled as I turned the steering wheel and eased into my driveway on the side farthest from the front door. "What kind of asshole parks closest to the entrance of someone else's house?" I huffed as I threw my car into park and killed the engine.

The driver's side door of the car was thrown open as I climbed out of mine, and in a second I had my answer.

"You have *got* to be kidding me," I seethed as I watched Oliver alight from the car and turn to give me the smile he had always thought was charming but I thought made him look like a douchebag from a tooth-paste commercial.

"Hi, sweetheart."

My exhaustion suddenly gave way to the kind of anger that usually led to women snapping and getting all sorts of stabby.

"What are you doing here, Oliver?"

He rounded his hood and started in my direction. "I've missed you so much. I wanted to surprise you. Aren't you happy to see me?"

My eyes bugged out wide. "Are you joking?" I shook my head, trying to wrap my brain around what the hell was happening. "How the hell did you find out where I live?"

"I had to pay a small fortune for the PI I hired, but every penny was worth it to see you."

"Jesus Christ, Oliver," I shouted. "What do I have to do to get it through your head that I don't want to see you? Do I need to file a restraining order?"

He grabbed my arm as I tried to pass him. "Look, Lennon, if we could just talk—"

I yanked my arm from his grip. "This is the last time I'm going to say this. You and I have *nothing* to talk about. We're done. The money you spent on that private investigator was wasted, because I never want to see you again. Go home."

I shouldered past him, heading for the front door. I slid my key in the lock quickly, but before I could slam the door in his face, he was there, shoving his way inside my house.

"What the hell are you doing? Get out of my house, Oliver."

He lifted his hands in a pleading gesture. "Five minutes. Please, baby. That's all I'm asking."

"Don't call me baby. I'm not your freaking baby." The endearment coming from him had always grated on my nerves, but now I hated it even more because that belonged to Pope.

"I'm sorry. I'm really sorry. I'm just asking for five minutes. Don't you think you owe me that much?"

I let out a caustic bark of laughter. "*Owe you*? I don't owe you a damn thing. That's the beautiful thing about divorce, it severs all ties you have with the other person."

"I didn't want the goddamn divorce in the first place," he shouted, throwing his arms in the air. "I tried to fight it, but you did it anyway!"

Something about his frantic demeanor made me stop and take a beat. I took him in for the first time since he showed up in my driveway, and as I looked at the man I'd spent so many years with, I struggled to find a single thing about him that might draw me in. I'd always thought he was handsome, but as I studied him just then, I couldn't for the life of me remember why. All I could do was compare him to Pope. I loved the easy way Pope wore a T-shirt and jeans so much more than the pressed slacks and button-down with the starched collar Oliver was currently wearing. I hated that his dark hair was probably stiff with the product he'd put in it earlier that morning so it would look perfect and the obnoxious gold watch on his wrist. I hated the smell of his cologne; that shit had always given me a headache, not that he cared.

There wasn't a single memory I could look back to that might cause a pang of longing in my chest. There were no lingering feelings of loss or sadness. The only thing I felt as I stood in front of the man I used to think I'd start a family and grow old with was annoyance that he was delaying my nice warm bath.

"I'm sorry you're still struggling with the divorce, but that's not my problem. If you really wanted to stay married, you shouldn't have gone around town sticking your dick in every willing woman who looked your way. Your parents should have taught you this a long time ago, but actions have consequences. And not being married to me anymore is your consequence."

His hands darted out, his fingers wrapping around mine and squeezing tightly. "I want you back, Lennon. I still love you."

I might have pitied the guy if I didn't know the truth. He didn't want *me* back, not the real me anyway. He wanted the version who did all the cooking and cleaning, the obedient little wife who'd wait on him hand and foot and not make waves. That wasn't who I really was, and I'd be damned if I'd go back to filling a role that never fit quite right. "That's not going to happen, Oliver. I'm sorry, but I don't feel the same way."

His expression turned pained as his grip tightened. "How can you say that? *We were married.* We made vows. You don't just stop loving a person overnight."

The hypocrisy he spouted was almost laughable. It was so ridiculous I couldn't be bothered to point it out to him. "Oliver, stop. Just stop," I urged as I pulled at my hands, trying to get him to let me go. "It's over, okay? I've met someone else."

He froze, his hold on my hands turning painfully tight as the color drained from his face. "You—you've met someone else?"

A bolt of uneasiness shot through me when I tried to extract my hands from his, but he wouldn't release his hold. "Oliver, let go."

The color returned to his face just as fast as it had drained out, but it was an ugly, mottled shade of red that made my heart beat faster. "You *met someone else?*" he hissed angrily.

Panic caused my chest to constrict as I yanked at my hands. "Oliver," I snapped, my tone as sharp as a whip cracking. "You need to let me go. Let me go and get the hell out of my house!"

He finally released me but then did something I never would have expected in a million years. Rearing back, he lifted his hand and swung, bringing his palm down on my cheek in a slap so hard it made me stumble to the side and bang into the wall as I tried to catch myself.

White starbursts exploded in front of my eyes while fire spread over my cheek, feeling like a million tiny ant bites.

I whipped my head back around to stare at him, gobsmacked into complete silence as I cradled my face where he'd just struck. He looked just as shocked as I felt, like he couldn't believe he'd just hit me.

"Oh my god, Lennon—"

He took a step in my direction, but I stumbled backward, trying to get away from him. "Don't come near me!" I shouted.

"Sweetheart, please. That was a mistake. I'm so sorry. I don't know what came over me. I can't believe I did that."

Oh, I knew what had come over him. His self-centered nature had finally come back to bite him in the ass. He was so used to getting what he wanted that when things weren't going his way, he lashed out in a way I never would have imagined.

"You stay the hell away from me, you unbelievable asshole! Get the fuck out of my house before I call the cops."

He held his hands up in surrender, slowly backing toward the front door. "I'm so sorry. You have to believe me."

"Get out!"

He tripped over his own feet at my outburst,

fumbling for the knob behind him. He finally got it open and stepped onto the threshold. "I'm going to make this right, sweetheart. You have my word. I'll fix this."

Before he could say another word, I slammed the door so fast he had to stumble backward to keep from getting hit by it, and fell right on his ass. I threw the deadbolt and added the chain lock, then I ran through the house, checking all the other doors and windows to make sure he didn't have another way inside before moving to the front window and peeking through the blinds. I watched as he backed out of my driveway, waiting until the car disappeared down the street before abandoning my post and rushing to the entryway where I'd dropped my purse on the floor.

My hands were shaking as I fished around inside for my phone. If this were any other town, I would have called the police to file a report against him, but after the stories I'd heard, I didn't trust them to handle the situation, so I dialed the number of the one person I trusted beyond all else.

I didn't realize I'd been holding my breath until his voice carried through the line, sinking beneath my skin and providing the comfort I so desperately needed just then.

"Hey, Raven. I was just about to call you. Left the garage earlier, and I'm headin' to pick up dinner right now. Should be there in about forty-five minutes."

I worried my bottom lip between my teeth, my face still burning like a lighter had been held to it. "Um, Pope? Can you come here instead?"

He went on alert immediately. "What's wrong?"

"Uh, so . . . my ex was just here."

That was all I needed to say. "I'll be there in ten. Keep the doors locked until I get there. You need me to stay on the phone with you?"

God, this man was so perfect.

"No," I whispered, my heart expanding in my chest until there was no room left. "I'm okay, baby. I just need you."

"You have me, Lennon. Always. I'll be right there."

It was on that declaration I knew I'd be fine. Because I had him, and that was all I needed.

TWENTY-TWO

POPE

MY HEART POUNDED SO GODDAMN HARD the entire way to Lennon's house, it was a wonder it hadn't beat its way right out of my chest and plummeted onto the road. I pushed my bike as hard as I could to get to my woman fast.

The ten minutes actually should have been more like fifteen, but when I heard her voice waver with fear, I knew I'd be flying through town to get to her. I made it in eight, and it was sheer luck that one of the asshole cops in this town hadn't spotted me shooting down the streets and tried to pull me over. Not that I would have stopped for them. I wasn't letting off the accelerator until I was at Lennon's, and that could have led to all kinds of shit I didn't have time to deal with since I needed to get to her.

The tension in my shoulders didn't begin to loosen

until I whipped my bike onto her street. I squealed my tires turning into her driveway, noticing she was parked on the wrong side, but I didn't stop to inspect why. I killed the engine and slammed the kickstand to the ground, then my boots ate up the distance to her front door.

It was yanked open the instant I started pounding on it, but it wasn't my woman who answered. Instead, I was standing face to face with Otto, the big man who lived next door.

"Son," he greeted, tilting his chin up at me and stepping aside. "She's fine. Just a little shaken up."

I appreciated him letting me know the state of things the moment I walked in, and since I didn't want to make it worse, I took a beat to close my eyes and focus on my breathing, counting down from ten. By the time I reached one, I felt more in control. Unfortunately, that feeling flew right out the fucking window when I stepped into the living room and found her sitting on that tiny fucking sofa with Esther, the older woman holding her soothingly as Lennon held a bag of frozen peas to her face.

"*He hit you*?" The words came out much harsher than I'd intended. I wanted to be her rock, the man who could comfort her, but that was proving hard as hell to do when all I saw was red. My blood was pounding in my ears, each beat sounding like it was saying *mur-der, mur-der*.

Lennon heaved out a weary sigh, lowering the bag of peas to her lap. Spread across her cheek was the bright red outline of a handprint. The moment I saw it, I knew one thing for certain. I was going to find that motherfucker and skin him alive.

And I'd have fun doing it.

She pushed off the couch and moved in my direction, the fire I was breathing clearly not intimidating her in the slightest. *Thank fuck.* That meant she felt safe with me, and I couldn't ask for anything better. She stopped in front of me, lifting to her tiptoes to press a gentle kiss to my lips. "Thank you for coming," she whispered, those soft words and that fucking handprint on her face nearly doing me in. The thought that someone had taken their hands to someone as beautiful, inside and out, as Lennon ripped at my insides, but instead of giving in to the beast that was demanding revenge, I wrapped my arms around her and pulled her into my chest. She immediately sank into me, nuzzling in deep on a contented sigh like this was all she needed to feel better.

This woman undid me.

"Always, Raven. You need me, I'll be here. Don't ever doubt that."

She pulled her head back and smiled. "I know."

I lowered my forehead to hers. "You okay?" It was

probably a stupid question, but I had to ask. I needed to know so that if she wasn't, I could do whatever she needed to get her to a better place.

"I'm fine. I just . . ." She pulled her lips between her teeth, the gesture almost nervous.

"Just what?"

"I don't want to stay here," she finally admitted. "Now that he knows where I live, it doesn't feel safe anymore."

I reached up, running my fingers through the hair at her temples all the way down to the ends. "Then it's a real good thing you're packing your stuff and going home with me."

Her entire face brightened at that. "Are you sure? I don't want to impose."

Like that would ever be possible. "I'm positive. We don't sleep apart, remember?" There hadn't been a night where she didn't sleep by my side since she finally stopped trying to fight the inevitable, and if I had my way, there never would be ever again.

She was mine.

"Come on, sweetie," Esther said as she came up beside Lennon and looped their arms together while offering me a warm smile. "I'll help you pack."

I watched as the two of them shuffled down the hall, waiting until I was sure they were out of earshot before I let out a string of curses under my breath.

I'd forgotten all about Otto until he came over and clapped his hand on my shoulder. "You'll be all right," he assured me. "So will she. You'll make sure of that."

I nodded, silently giving the man who thought of Lennon as family my word that I would see to it that she was okay.

His eyes bored into mine. "And if you're the man I think you are, you'll make that son of a bitch pay for putting his hands on her."

"That's a fuckin' guarantee," I gritted out.

"Good." His hand on my shoulder clenched. "And make sure you make it hurt."

Oh, I had every intention.

I stood outside the door of the master bathroom, listening as Lennon hummed a tune I couldn't make out as the water ran, filling the tub for the bubble bath she'd requested the moment I got her back to my place.

She seemed fine, for the most part, but I was still struggling with that raging monster inside of me who was desperate to get out and rain down hell on that piece of shit. I'd given Otto my word I'd make him pay, and I planned on doing just that.

While she relaxed in the tub with a glass of wine—I made sure to keep it stocked since it seemed to be her go-to after a long day—and her e-reader, I went about emptying a couple drawers in my dresser and moving things around in my closest to make room for her. Then I unpacked her bags, because now that I had her here, I fully intended to keep her. I wanted my place to be our place, and I didn't care how crazy that seemed or if I was moving too fast. I was doing what felt right, and bringing Lennon's personality into this space in any way she wanted *felt right*.

She still hadn't managed to purchase any furniture or knickknacks for her house—a point in my favor. It was a great house, sure. But every time I was there, it felt like it was more of a stopover to something else for her. An empty one at that. She didn't treat it like it was forever.

I'd let her redo every room in my house if that was what she wanted. Anything to make her happy. She said there were no pieces of her in her old house, so I wanted her to fill this place up. I wanted to see her and feel her everywhere.

After I finished getting her stuff unpacked, I moved back to the door and pressed my ear close before knocking.

Her melodic voice called from the other side of the heavy wood. "It's your bathroom, honey. You don't have to knock."

I wanted to correct her, tell her I wanted it to be *our* bathroom, but that was a conversation for another time. First I had to talk her around to what was about to go down and hope like hell it didn't freak her out.

I pushed the door open and moved into the bathroom, breathing in the thick, steamy air that smelled like her. Her skin was flushed and dewy from the hot water and her hair was bunched up at the top of her head. She smiled and it was like a punch to the gut. Christ, she was beautiful.

I couldn't wrap my head around the fact that the most important men in her life had treated her so carelessly. They'd obviously been too stupid to realize the treasure they held in their hands, but I wasn't going to make the same mistake. Their loss was my gain, and I would make sure to spend every day proving I intended to care for her in all the ways her father and ex had failed to do.

"Hey. I'm in love with your bathtub. I think I might just move in here."

It took some effort, but I managed to crack a smile of my own. "No need to go to those extremes. You're welcome to use it whenever you want."

Her smile slipped a little, her head canting to the side as she studied me. "Is everything okay? You seem tense."

"That's what I want to talk to you about." I sat on the edge of the tub, reaching out to run the pads of my fingers across her jaw. "Some of my guys are on their way right now. I'm gonna leave one here with you, just to keep an eye out, make sure you're safe."

Her brows scrunched together. "Where will you be?"

I pulled a deep breath in through my nose. "My guy Bane tracked down where your ex is staying. We're going to pay him a visit."

Her eyes went wide and she sat up fast, sloshing the water around the tub. "Pope, no. You can't—"

"I have to. That man came into your home uninvited. He made you feel unsafe, and he put his goddamn hands on you," I finished on a growl, barely containing the rage I felt when I thought back to that handprint on her cheek and what she'd told me of the interaction. "He hit you, Raven. He has to pay for that."

She closed her eyes and pressed her uninjured cheek into my palm like she wanted to get lost in my touch. I gave that to her. Hell, there wasn't anything I *wouldn't* give her. I waited until those sea foam eyes of hers opened, shining with worry before she turned and placed a kiss in the center of my palm.

"I don't want you to do anything that might get you or your guys in trouble. He's not worth it, Pope."

That was where she was very wrong. If it meant keeping her safe, it was worth it. I'd set the world on fire, throw gasoline on the flames, and enjoy a cold beer while I watched it burn to the ground.

I didn't stop the grin that pulled at my lips. "You don't need to worry about that. No one will ever know it was us."

It hadn't taken long for Bane to track the motherfucker down, and just like I knew he would be, Oliver Banion was the very definition of a coward. One look at me and my guys, and he'd nearly shit himself in fear.

It had taken hardly any effort to gag and blindfold him before tossing him in the back of a van and carting his ass to our clubhouse. No one had been down there in some time, but there was a room in the basement we used to use when we needed to make a point, or worse, eliminate a threat, then work on getting rid of the body.

I hadn't been down in this room since we'd dragged Greaser's ass here, the member we'd kicked out then had to take care of after he stole from us and started stirring up all kinds of trouble.

I might have been itching to end this guy's life tonight, that old part of me scratching at my insides, begging to be let out, but I knew if I crossed that line, Lennon would never look at me the same way again.

So instead of killing him and burying him out in the

foothills somewhere his body would never be found, I'd settled on making the bastard suffer to the point he'd *wish* he was dead.

He let out a whimper as I moved to the table and tossed down the bloody pliers I'd been using.

"Please," he begged, his words garbled thanks to the molars I'd just finished ripping out of his mouth. Tears ran down his cheeks and mixed with the blood from the beating I'd given him. Brass knuckles worked wonders in turning a grown man's face into ground beef.

We had him strapped to a wooden chair, his wrists and ankles bound with duct tape. The front of his expensive-ass pants were soaked with urine, and I was positive I'd broken several of his ribs. I'd really put the work in to make sure this guy hurt as my men watched on without so much as batting an eye. We'd all seen worse. Hell, it had been a long time, but we'd all done worse. When my brothers found out this prick had hit Lennon, they hadn't hesitated to roll out with me. She was mine, which, in their eyes, made her family.

Bane was sitting at a rickety table in the corner of the room, typing away on his laptop. Roe stood with his back against the wall beside us, using a fucking eight-inch Bowie knife to clean his nails while another one of my guys, Rake, sat cleaning his gun. Intimidation tactics, but they'd worked like a charm.

"Please, just stop. I'll do whatever you want. You want money? I'll give you money. Just let me go."

I wiped his blood off my hands before tossing the towel aside. "You think that's why we're doing this? Because we want money?"

Roe chuckled darkly, the blade of his knife glinting underneath the overhead light. "Pretty sure I got more money in my wallet than this pissant has in his fuckin' bank account."

"Then what do you want?" he sobbed, dropping his head as I moved closer, leaning down so I was at eye level with him.

"What I want is to make you suffer for putting your hands on my woman."

He whipped his head back up, his one good eye bugging out. The other had already swollen completely shut. "It's you?" He wheezed. "You're the guy—"

"Yep. It's me. I'm the guy who swooped in after you were too goddamn stupid to realize what you had. I'm the guy who fucks her so good she's already addicted to my cock. And I'm the guy who gives her what she wants and needs and taught her what it's like to be with a real man. Lennon's mine, and you put your hands on her." I reached out, clapping him on the shoulder roughly, causing him to whimper as I jostled his shattered ribs. "See, I can't sit back and let what you did stand. This is your punishment, not only for hitting her, but for also refusin' to leave her alone, even though she told you she was done with you."

"I'll leave her alone," he cried. "I swear! She'll never see or hear from me again!"

My chest shook on a low chuckle. "Oh, I already know that." Turning to look at Bane over my shoulder, I asked, "You got everything you need?"

The smile he shot me bordered on psycho. "I got it. Address, banking and retirement account numbers. Even got what I need to take down daddy's little company. Bet the SEC would have a field day."

Lennon's ex choked. "You can't . . ."

"And I won't. At least not right now. But if you ever try to contact Lennon again, if you so much as *think* about her, or if you get the crazy idea you'll go to the cops and tell them what happened here, I won't hesitate to set your entire fuckin' world on fire. You get me?"

His head bobbled back and forth. "I understand. I swear. I won't say a word to anyone."

"Good." Pushing up, I headed back to the table and reached for the pliers I'd discarded earlier. I believed he'd keep his mouth shut and leave my woman alone. But I wasn't quite done working my anger out.

TWENTY-THREE

LENNON

WRAPPED in one of Pope's long, fluffy towels, I drained the tub and moved to the mirror, wiping away the condensation that had built up from my long, hot bath. I'd refilled it twice, content to simply soak in the water and rinse the day away.

As I took in my reflection, leaning closer to the glass to inspect my cheek, I was happy to see there was no lasting damage. No swelling or serious bruising, but a faint mark remained that I could easily cover with makeup, so I wouldn't have to call in to work until it healed.

I expected to be more upset than I actually was. Sure, I was pissed as hell that my ex-husband had basically stalked me then slapped me in the face when he didn't get his way, and maybe in the light of day, the events of this evening would finally crash into me, but I wasn't feeling the stress just then. Maybe it was the wine Pope had poured me or the bubble bath he'd drawn. Or maybe it was the man himself, a man who'd proven at every turn he'd have my back, that made me feel better. Instead of holding on to what had happened and replaying it over and over, I was content to let it go.

Moving into the bedroom, I looked around for my suitcases, but they weren't on the far side of the room where I'd left them. I pulled the closet door open and found them against the wall, empty.

My chest expanded on a sharp gasp when I looked up and noticed my clothes hanging across from Pope's, my shoes lined on the shelf above. On a hunch, I moved out of the closet and over to the chest of drawers that butted up against the wall across from the bed. Sure enough, when I slid the first drawer open, I found my underwear and sleep clothes. The second drawer contained my T-shirts and shorts.

My eyes began to sting as I stared at my clothes. While I'd been relaxing, he was making room for me in his home and unpacking my stuff, an action that spoke volumes on how much he wanted me here.

A giddy smile pulled at my face, making my cheek ache a bit, as I rummaged through the drawer for a pair of sleep shorts and a matching tank, then I went back into the closet, pulling one of Pope's flannel shirts off its hanger and sliding it on. I cuffed the sleeves, leaving it unbuttoned as I grabbed the collar and lifted it to my nose, sniffing deeply.

It smelled just like him, and the warmth of having it wrapped around me was almost as good as being in his arms. *Almost.*

It wasn't until my stomach let out an unhappy growl that I remembered, in the chaos of everything that had happened, I'd completely forgotten to eat.

Heading out of the room, I padded down the hall toward the kitchen, my mind set on making a BLT, when I jerked to a stop and let out a startled squeak at the sight of a man sitting on the couch.

"Oh my god," I cried, clutching at my heart.

"Sorry, sweetheart. Thought Pope told you I'd be here."

The man looked to be in his late sixties to early seventies, wearing wire-rimmed glasses and sitting on the couch with what looked like a paperback western novel in his hands.

"No, he did. Sorry, I must have forgotten." I moved closer to him, extending my hand. "Hi. I'm Lennon."

His smile was warm and full of kindness as he took my hand and gave it a hearty shake. "Know who you are, darlin'. We all do. Everyone's been talkin' about how Pope's sprung for Snow White."

I let out a snort. "Snow White?"

"That's the nickname that's been goin' around the

club since the night you two met. We've all been itchin' to meet you. Glad I get to be the first. Everybody calls me Pops."

My cheeks heated at the news that my relationship with Pope was so widely discussed among his club. I returned his infectious grin, throwing my thumb over my shoulder. "Well, Pops, I was just about to make myself a sandwich. Since it seems you're stuck on babysitting duty, how about you join me?"

He clapped the book shut and tossed it onto the cushion next to him. "Know what? Wouldn't mind if I do." He rose to his considerable height and extended his arm for me to lead the way.

"You want anything to drink?" I offered. "Beer, water . . ."

"Beer would be nice, sweetheart, but I can get it." He headed for the fridge and pulled out a bottle, lifting it my way in a silent question. I waved him off, already feeling the effects of the wine I drank on an empty stomach while I was in the bath.

As I rummaged through the fridge for everything I needed to make a couple BLTs, Pops pulled up one of the stools at the island and made himself comfortable. Pope's fridge was *way* better stocked than mine. I pulled out a packet of bacon and a skillet, getting slices started before moving to the cutting board and slicing through a juicy tomato and a crisp head of iceberg lettuce. "So how long have you known Pope?" I asked, suddenly eager for any information I could get.

"Oh, his whole life. His old man and I were friends since we were kids ourselves, so I was there for all of it. When he and Pope's mom got married, when all three kids were born."

"Pope has another sibling?" I knew about a sister because of Marigold, but he'd never mentioned another sibling.

"Oh, yeah. A younger half-brother. Unfortunately they aren't that close. Last I heard, he's livin' somewhere in Montana."

I flipped the bacon in the skillet, eager for more of the story. "Pope never mentioned a half-brother or stepmom."

Pops lifted his shoulder in a shrug. "Suppose he wouldn't. That marriage didn't last long. It was more of a rebound sort of thing for Court. His first wife, Camille, Pope's mother, was the love of his life. It was a sad, sad day when she lost her battle with breast cancer. Pope and Angela were still little, and Court was all kinds of lost without her. Nancy came in his life when he was drownin'. Woman loved Court like mad. Tried her hardest to fill the void Cammy left behind, but when you've already met the one, no one else really compares. Nan finally realized she'd always come in second to a ghost, and decided she deserved better. Can't say I blame her, honestly. Anyway, she packed up her and Court's son and moved on to Montana."

My heart clenched at that story. It broke my heart to think of a young Pope lost and adrift without his mother, and of his heartbroken father trying to find his way in the world without the woman he cherished.

"You know, since we're bein' honest here, I've been half convinced that boy was going to spend his whole life alone, never bein' tied down. But then I see the look on his face when he's talkin' about you, and it's just how Court used to look at his Camille. Gotta say, it puts my old heart at ease, knowing he finally found himself somethin' like that."

I couldn't help the goofy smile that tugged at my lips as I transferred the bacon from the pan to a plate. "I think Pope's amazing. I've never . . . well, I've never had anyone treat me the way he does. He makes me feel . . . special. Cherished. He's important to me."

Pops reached across the counter, stopping me as I assembled our sandwiches to place his hand on top of mine. "Then it warms my heart even more knowin' my boy's finally giving you the good you deserve as well."

"You know what, Pops? I think you and I are going to get along beautifully."

He chuckled deeply and lifted his beer in salute. "I think you're right."

I woke to Pope's fingers brushing against my forehead as he pushed my hair away from my face. After Pops and I ate our BLTs, I had another glass of wine while we sat on the couch and got to know each other, talking and laughing until the alcohol finally got on top of me and I struggled to keep my eyes open. Pops eventually ordered me to bed, and I'd been too tired to argue. I passed out almost as soon as my head hit the pillow.

I blinked my eyes open, taking in the man hovering over me. The sky outside was still black, so I couldn't have been asleep for long. "Hey," I said quietly, pushing myself up to sitting as a huge yawn stretched my jaw wide. "What time is it?"

His expression softened as he smiled down at me. "Late. You should go back to sleep. I didn't mean to wake you."

"That's okay." I looked him over, checking for any signs of what might have happened while he was with Oliver. My heartbeat sped up at the sight of his bruised knuckles, but otherwise, he didn't look out of sorts. "Is, um, everything okay?"

The mattress sank beneath his weight as he sat down beside me. His hand came up, his fingers wrapping gently around my throat so he could use his thumb to tip my chin up and press his lips to mine. "It's all good, Raven."

"Is he . . ." My throat worked on a swallow. But as if reading my mind, he answered before I had to finish my question.

"He's alive. He's just in serious pain right now. But he's never going to be a problem for you again."

I leaned deeper into his touch, closing my eyes as I breathed out a sigh of relief that this whole nightmare with Oliver was over.

"You're pretty incredible, you know that?"

"I'm just me, baby." He might be playing it like it wasn't a big deal, but he'd done more for me in the short time we'd known each other than anyone else had my entire life. It might have seemed like no big deal to him, but to me it meant everything.

"You know, I noticed you basically moved me in here," I said in a teasing voice, expecting him to smile or laugh. "If you aren't careful, I might get too comfortable and end up staying."

But he didn't, instead, he nodded solemnly. "I'm okay with that. I want you all over this house," he stated seriously. "If it's too soon for you, I'll help you pack it all back up, but you should know, I want you here. I want you to leave your mark everywhere. You're it for me, and

I know it might feel like it's too soon, but I have to be honest with you."

My lips parted, my lungs filling with a huge inhale. "Pope."

"I've never felt this way before. I'm all in. You're it for me baby."

My entire face split on a huge grin. "I'm all in too," I admitted, giddiness coursing through my veins, making my insides feel all fizzy. "And I'd love to stay here with you. If that's what you want."

"It's what I want," he answered instantly. "Then it's settled. I'll have the guys handle packing up the rest of your stuff and move you in here officially."

A giggle burst past my lips as he moved in, taking me to my back and hovering over me, his lips coming down on mine in a hungry kiss. "Funny, I don't feel tired all of a sudden."

He gave me a wicked grin. "Is that right? What do you think we should do then?"

The answer to that was easy. "I think we should celebrate. Naked."

TWENTY-FOUR

POPE

I PUSHED OPEN the door to the office and stepped inside, a spring in my step as I headed for the coffee pot.

"Mornin' old man," I greeted Pops as I poured that sludge into a cup. My mood was so damn good I didn't even taste the shitty burnt coffee.

"Well look at you," Pops said teasingly, pulling off his glasses as he sat back in the chair behind the desk. "Looks like someone woke up on the right side of the bed this mornin'."

As long as Lennon was in that bed with me, there was no such thing as a wrong side. It had been two days since she had officially moved in with me, and I didn't think it was possible to be happier than I currently was.

I held my arms out at my sides. "What can I say? Life's pretty fuckin' good right now."

The door leading into the garage opened, and Roe

came walking in dressed in a pair of coveralls with the sleeves tied at his waist and a gray tee. "You talkin' about Prez walking around like he's farting daisies and shittin' rainbows?"

I laughed at his description, feeling so damn good I didn't mind being razzed. "Hey man, don't be pissed I got a good woman at home and you're stuck in that cold bed all alone."

He pulled a bottle of water from the mini fridge in the corner and shot me a smirk before taking a drink. "Bed didn't feel too cold this mornin' when I was balls deep in the chick I picked up from the bar last night while my face was buried in her friend's pussy."

I'd had more than my fair share of wild nights over the years. They just went hand in hand with the lifestyle we led. But I wouldn't trade what I currently had with one perfect woman for any of that bullshit if you paid me.

I chuckled, shaking my head as I took a sip of coffee and thought of how hilarious it was going to be to watch my closest friend fall ass over elbow for the right woman when she finally came along.

I looked back to Pops and noticed for the first time that his complexion was off. He looked pale, and his eyes had taken on a glassiness that wasn't normal for the man who usually didn't miss anything.

"Hey, you good old man?"

He mopped at the sweat on his forehead with his ever-present handkerchief. "All good. Just a bit of indigestion this mornin'," he said as he massaged the center of his chest like he was trying to relieve a pain.

Roe came up beside me, concern clear in his expression as he took in the man who was like a father to both of us. While I'd had my old man for the better part of my life, Roe's father was a piece of shit with a penchant for using his fists more often than his words. Roe had taken off, running away from home when he was still a teenager, and it had been my dad and Pops who had taken him in, guiding him onto a better path than the one he'd been on. Pops had been the closest thing he had to a real father, and when he became old enough, he'd prospected with me to follow in his footsteps and become an Iron Wraith.

"You sure? You don't look so hot. Maybe we should get you to a doctor."

He tried waving us off like everything was fine, but the sweating was getting worse, and he was clutching his arm. "I'm fine. Probably just overdid it with the pizza last night."

Christ, that man's diet was going to be the death of him.

It was on that thought that he tried standing, making it all of one step before clutching at his arm and collapsing onto floor with a pained groan.

"Fuck!" I barked as Roe and I rushed around the desk, panic gripping at my insides like an ice-cold fist.

I hit my knees beside Pops, struggling to lift the man's weight as I looked at Roe and barked, *"Call an ambulance!"*

I couldn't lose Pops. The *club* couldn't lose him. He was our glue. The moral compass who had helped me through some of the darkest days of my life. I would *not* lose him.

Lennon

I watched the clock, waiting for the bell to ring. With each passing minute, my anxiety got worse. It was bad enough Pope still hadn't answered my earlier texts, but Marigold's absence the past two mornings had my stomach twisted into knots.

Finally, class ended, and the kids shot from their seats before the bell had finished ringing.

I rounded my desk, my eyes on the two girls I always saw Marigold with. "Hannah, Reagan, have either of you seen Marigold?"

The girls looked at each other, a whole conversation communicated through their eyes. "Uh, no. We haven't seen her since Wednesday," Hannah answered before pulling her bottom lip between her teeth and biting down.

That was the same day I'd confronted her. "Well, have you spoken to her? She was complaining about a cold. Is she still sick?"

They shared another look, and it took everything in me to keep from screaming. Finally, Reagan shook her head. "No, Ms. Cody. We've called her like, a million times, but she hasn't answered."

"She, um . . ," Hannah shifted from foot to foot anxiously, twisting her fingers together in front of her. "She wouldn't tell us what's been going on, but she said there was some stuff happening with her mom."

My stomach sank as my heart started beating faster, but I did my best to hide my reaction behind a wobbly smile. "All right. Thanks, girls. You should get to your next class."

They disappeared, and as students filtered in for their next period, I moved back to my desk, picked up my phone, and opened my texts. The last one I'd sent Pope, asking if he'd spoken to Marigold, still sat unanswered and unread. Instead of typing out another, I scrolled to his contact and hit go, bringing it up to my ear. It rang and rang before going straight to voicemail, and I had to swallow the curse that wanted to break through as I hung up without leaving a message.

Phoebe came into my classroom just then. We still had a couple minutes before the kids had to be in their seats, so she headed straight for me.

"She's not here again?" she asked, speaking about Marigold.

I shook my head, nibbling nervously on my thumbnail. "No. She was absent again. I asked her friends if they've talked to her, but they said she's been radio silent for the past two days."

I saw concern melting into her features. It was normal for a student to be sick, sure, but these kids were practically fused to their phones, texting their friends at all hours of the day and night. To have a fourteen-year-old girl go quiet on her best friends wasn't only unusual, it was extremely troubling.

"What did Pope say?"

I shook my head, my chest feeling tighter and tighter by the second. "He's not answering texts or calls. I don't know where the hell he is."

Sensing my panic, Phoebe brought her hands up in a soothing gesture. "Okay. It's okay. Just take a breath." I copied what she did, pulling a deep breath in through my nose and slowly blowing it out past my lips. "I'm sure she's fine. She's probably in bed sleeping off a cold or something. You have a free period after this, right?" I nodded. "Then I say you take that time and go check on her, see for yourself that she's all right."

I could have smacked myself in the forehead for not thinking of that sooner. "You don't think that's too intrusive?"

Phoebe shook her head. "Nope, not if it provides you some relief. But maybe hit her other classes and get the assignments she's missed the past couple days as a cover. If her mom's there, you can say you were dropping them off so she didn't fall behind."

"You're a genius, you know that?"

Phoebe's grin was cocky as she planted her hands on her hips and preened. "Well, it's about time you realized." She turned serious then. "Everything is going to be fine. Just get through this period and you'll be able to see for yourself."

God, I hoped she was right. Because I couldn't shake the dark, sinking feeling in the pit of my stomach that something was wrong.

TWENTY-FIVE

LENNON

I'D CALLED Pope three more times after leaving school on my free period, but I still wasn't getting through. I pulled up to the small house listed as Marigold's home address, taking in the front yard full of dead grass and overgrown weeds. The windows were dingy, and the screens were either caked in dirt or rotted and torn. And from my vantage point at the street, I could see the roof was missing several shingles. My heart tugged at the thought of this place being where such a sweet, bright, girl was forced to live. It was clear the owner of the place had neglected it, letting it fall into disrepair. I shouldn't have been surprised, though. After all, if a woman could be so careless as to forget to pick up her own child, I doubted housework was high on her priority list.

I didn't know much about Pope's sister, Angela, but what little he'd shared had put my teeth on edge. I had always tried not to judge other people until I got to know them for myself, but I could say with certainty, after the stories I'd heard and the tears I'd witnessed in Marigold's eyes that first day, I did *not* like this woman.

Parking my car, I took a deep, calming breath, and pulled the stack of coursework I'd gathered from Marigold's teachers out of my messenger bag. My heels clicked on the walkway's broken concrete as I made my way to the front door. As I got closer, I heard sounds coming from inside. The blinds on the front window were pulled shut, preventing me from seeing in as I stopped at the door.

I lifted my hand and knocked, straining to hear anything over the TV that blared inside. I waited, hoping someone would answer, but as the seconds ticked by, there was nothing. I knocked again, this time calling out, "Ms. Pope? My name is Lennon Cody. I'm one of Marigold's teachers." Still nothing, so I decided to bang. "Ms. Pope? Can you hear me?"

Tingles traveled up my spine, making the tiny hairs on the back of my neck stand on end, it was my body's way of telling me something wasn't right, an internal alarm I couldn't ignore. Instead of backing away, I reached for the knob. I knew I had no business entering someone else's house without permission, but the tiny voice in the back of my head was screaming that Marigold was in trouble. I had to do something. I wouldn't have been able to live with myself if I ignored this feeling and found out later that something terrible had happened.

So on a deep inhale, I twisted, my shoulders slumping in relief when the knob turned and the door pushed open.

"Ms. Pope?" I called as I slowly stepped across the threshold. "Marigold? It's Ms. Cody. Anyone here?" From what I could see from the muted sunlight fighting its way through the closed blinds, the living room looked like it had been hit by a tornado. It wasn't just the mess of beer cans and empty liquor bottles either. The coffee table was broken on the floor and shattered glass from broken picture frames crunched beneath the soles of my shoes.

A cold sweat broke out on the back of my neck. It felt like someone had reached right into my chest and squeezed as hard as they could. A chill ran over my entire body as I moved to the television, feeling around until I found the power button and shut it off. "Angela?" I called again, my voice sounding frantic. "Marigold?"

I froze when I heard the faintest sound coming from the back of the house, not moving an inch or daring to breathe as I waited for it again so I could figure out where it was coming from. As soon as I heard it the second time, I took off, running down the hallway, crunching on more broken glass from the frames that had been knocked off the walls. The first door was open, but there was no one there. The sheets on the queen-sized bed were rumpled and spilling onto the floor, but other than more empty bottles and cans, this room wasn't nearly in as bad a shape. The next door was to an empty bathroom, so I kept running, my heart lodged firmly in my throat.

"Marigold!" I cried as I skidded to a stop at the last door at the end of the hall. This room was painted in shades of pink with posters and photographs of Marigold and her friends taped to the walls, clearly her room. Unlike the other one, this bedroom was trashed. The dresser had been pushed over onto its front. Makeup and perfume bottles that had been on top were smashed on the dingy carpet. The chair that matched the flimsy dresser resting against the back wall was in pieces, and the mirror hanging above it was smashed. This room looked even worse than the living room. Whatever nightmare had happened in this house started in this room then carried throughout.

The bed frame for the twin bed had been broken, leaving it lopsided and off center, and there, in the center of the mattress, curled up in a tiny ball, was the woman

I'd seen pick Marigold up from school in the afternoons. Angela.

After that first day, I'd taken to watching from my classroom window to make sure Pope's niece was picked up safely every day, and I'd made sure to memorize the woman's face. Only, at that moment, it was swollen and covered in dried blood and dark purple bruises.

"Oh my god!" I cried as I rushed to the bed, dropping to my knees.

Angela peeled one eye open—only able to lift it part way due to the swelling. "He took her," she muttered, her voice so small she sounded more like a terrified child than a grown woman. "She's gone."

"Who's gone?" I pressed frantically. "Marigold? Is Marigold gone?"

"He took her. Took my little girl," she continued. "And I let him."

"Who, Angela? Who took her?"

"I let him take her. I just let him. I couldn't stop him."

My composure snapped and I grabbed hold of her shoulders, shaking her violently. "Listen to me!" I shouted in the woman's face, not feeling the slightest twinge of guilt when she cried out in pain. "Where's Marigold? Who took her?"

"Wilfred," she said on a sob. "Grant Wilfred. I—I was working for him."

I released her and grabbed my cell from the back pocket of my slacks. "I have to call the police."

"No!" Angela lunged then, wrapping her hand around my wrist and squeezing it tighter than I would have thought her capable of. "You can't call the cops."

"We need to find her!"

"Wilfred's a cop. He's dirty. They're *all* dirty."

Dear Lord. She'd been working with a cop she *knew* was dirty?

I felt my eyes heat with a fresh wave of tears. I felt helpless and terrified, but I couldn't panic. There was no time to curl up in a ball like Angela had done. I had to act, and if the cops couldn't help, I knew someone who could.

"Come on. Get up." I shot to my feet, grabbing Angela and yanking her roughly off the bed. "We have to go."

"Where?"

"We're going to Pope. He'll get her back." I'd never been surer of anything in all my life. That man would move heaven and earth for that girl, and God forgive anyone who got in his way.

"He's gonna be so mad at me," Angela sobbed. "He'll hate me forever."

"Look at me," I barked, jerking on her arm until her swollen, watery gaze met mine. "This isn't about you.

This is about *her*. So you're going to pull yourself together and be the mother that girl needs. And once we have her back safely, you can worry about how your brother feels about you, but until then. It's. About. *Her.* Now let's go."

My tires squealed as I slammed on my brakes in front of the garage, shoving the gearshift into park and throwing my door open. I was hit with a new wave of panic as I looked at the garage, seeing that the doors on every bay were pulled closed, padlocks securing them in place. It didn't look like a soul was there, but I refused to give up. Running toward the door marked *office*, I rushed up the stairs and pounded on the glass, ignoring the closed sign that hung in the window.

"Hello?" I shouted as I continued beating on the door. "Hello, is anyone here?"

"Can I help you with somethin'?"

I whipped around at the sound of the unfamiliar voice and spotted a man standing at the other building across the lot from the garage. He looked a bit younger than Pope, but I knew by the vest he was wearing over his white tee, he was one of his brothers. A fellow Wraith.

I ran down the steps in his direction, my heart racing with each pounding step of my high heels against the concrete. "I need Pope," I insisted desperately. "Is Pope here?"

The man's brows went up at my frantic demeanor. "He's not—" He stopped, squinting at me as I got closer. "Snow White?"

I remembered Pops using that nickname a few nights ago and him explaining that was how a lot of these guys referred to me. "Yes. Please. You have to help me. Is Pope here?"

"He's not, darlin'. He's at the hospital." When my eyes threatened to bug out of my chest, he held his hands up to explain. "Pops had a heart attack." *Oh god, no.* "He's in surgery right now, and they expect him to be all right, but the Prez and a few of the others went with him. What's goin' on? Is it your ex?" He caught sight of movement behind me and looked over my shoulder. "Holy shit. Is that Angela? What the fuck happened?"

"It's Marigold," I managed to say around the lump of cement that had formed in my throat. "Someone— someone took her."

His nostrils flared and something moved over his face, something that shook me right down to my very soul. In the blink of an eye, this man went from calm and collected to downright terrifying, and if I hadn't been so desperate to get Marigold back, I probably would have turned and run away. But I steeled my spine and forced myself to stay put.

"Come with me. I know how to reach your man."

Oh thank god. I just hoped it wasn't too late.

TWENTY-SIX

POPE

I PACED the length of the hospital waiting room like a caged lion, thirsty to escape and rip someone's throat out.

We spoke to the doc once already, and he'd been confident that after a surgery to fix a couple blockages, that Pops would be back on his feet in no time, but the fist that had been squeezing my heart in a vice grip since the old man went down hadn't loosened up. He had to be okay. There was no other acceptable outcome. If that man died on me, I'd find a way to get to him wherever he was and kick his ass.

I vaguely heard the sound of a phone ringing, and the rumble of Roe's voice as he answered, but I was so lost in my own head that I couldn't make out what he was saying. It sounded like it was coming from the other side of a long, dark tunnel.

Movement from the corner of my eyes caught my attention, and I turned to look just as Roe shot to his feet and charged in my direction.

"We gotta go."

My chin jerked back in shock. "What? Why? What's goin' on?"

His nostrils flared on a deep breath, his eyes dark and dangerous. Then he opened his mouth and spoke, stripping the world right out from beneath my feet. "Your woman just showed up at the clubhouse with your sister in tow. Bane said Angela's been beat to shit, and . . ." His throat worked on a swallow. "Your niece has been taken, brother." My lungs seized and he clamped a hand down on my shoulder, partly for support but also to keep me from losing my shit and ripping this place apart. "Don't have the full story. Just know Ang somehow got involved with Grant Wilfred and things went south. He beat the hell out of her and took Marigold as payment for somethin'."

That was all I could stand to hear. Shoving his arm off me, I started out of the waiting room, barely hearing as my VP and best friend ordered a few of the guys to stay there for Pops while he told the others to come with us.

I barely remembered the ride back to the clubhouse from the hospital, my men on their bikes behind me. It felt like it took an eternity to get there while also only the blink of an eye. By the time I pulled into the forecourt, a line of bikes was stretched across the chain link fence. Bane had been busy in the short time it took me to get here. It looked like almost every brother was here to have my back.

My footsteps beat against the concrete as I rushed to the clubhouse, grabbing the handle to the door and ripping it open.

It took my eyes a second to adjust to the change in lighting, but the instant they did, the first thing I saw was my Raven.

She jumped up from the barstool she was sitting on a rushed to me, throwing herself in my arms as soon as she got close enough. I pulled her flush to my chest and held on tight. She was my port in the storm just then, the only guiding light I had through the darkness that was threatening to swallow me up.

Sensing I needed her strength, she pulled back and reached up to cradle my face in her delicate hands. "You'll find her," she said, like it was already a foregone conclusion. I swallowed, my throat feeling like it had been rubbed raw with sandpaper. "You'll find her," she repeated, her voice firmer, leaving no room for argument. "Because you're a *good man*, Pope, and good men win. You'll get her back, and together, we'll make sure she spends the rest of her life happy and safe."

Goddamn right we would.

I nodded, letting her go as she pulled away and turning my focus to Bane standing right behind her.

"Where the fuck is she?" I growled, murder coating my words.

He jerked his chin over his shoulder and stepped aside, revealing a bruised and beaten Angela sitting on one of the old, tattered couches we had shoved up against a wall. One of her eyes was swollen completely shut, the other not much better, but it still managed to widen in fear at the sight of me. There was one moment where my heart sank at the sight of her. Just one single moment. But then I remembered what Roe had said. My Goldie was missing, and it was all her fault. Any sympathy I might have been feeling at seeing her hurt withered and died under that truth.

I latched onto Lennon's hand and towed her along with me as I shoved past everyone else and went to confront my sister.

"Talk," I barked hard and loud enough to make her jolt. "*Now*."

She flinched at my voice, but didn't make me wait. "When you cut me off, I didn't know what to do. I didn't have a job, and there was no money, so I reached out to some of Jeff's buddy's and started asking about work that might make me some fast cash."

Jesus fucking Christ.

"Turns out, Jeff was workin' for Wilfred. When you

ran him out of town, that opened up a spot. I jumped through hoops to get a face to face with him, and he brought me in on his operation."

"To deal for him." It wasn't a question. If my sister was involved, I already knew without having to ask what they were up to.

She nodded, sniffling as a tear spilled from her eye and tracked down her cheek. I didn't feel even the slightest bit of sadness for her.

"So you were dealin' pills and god knows what else for this fucker, and somethin' went wrong. What was it?"

"I, well . . ." She cleared her throat, that one good eye darting around and looking anywhere but at me. "I took some of the pills for myself. I was going to pay for them, I swear!" she rushed out. "But you said you were done with me, that you wouldn't give me another dime—"

I held my hand up to silence her, barely hanging on by a thread.

"How long ago did he take her?"

A sob broke from her throat. "Y-yesterday."

I had to curl my free hand into a tight fist to keep from raging, and as if sensing I was only seconds from losing it, my Raven reached up and placed her hand on my chest, her touch somehow soothing the beast that was roaring to life inside me, at least for the time being. That monster had had her for more than twenty-four hours. And the only reason I knew it had happened was because my woman had sensed something was wrong and went to track her down.

"Where did he take her?"

"I-I don't know. I swear."

I moved then, so fast it startled her. One second I was hovering over her, the next I was pulling her up by her arm and in her face, my fury filling every single spare inch of the room around us. "You better think really fuckin' hard. This is happening because of *you*. I don't have time to stand here and listen to your bullshit excuses while that piece of shit is out there with *my girl*. So you're gonna tell me right fuckin' now, *where did he take her?*"

"He—he has a place," she sputtered. "I don't know the exact location, all I know is it's in the foothills somewhere about an hour north of here. I've only been there once. It's where—"

When she stopped, I jerked her by her arm hard enough to make her head snap back. "It's what?"

"It's where he meets with the men *he* works for." Her features blanketed with panic as she reached up she clutched at the front of my shirt. "You have to get her back, Pope. Please, I'm beggin' you. These guys . . . they're *bad* guys. If Wilfred gives her to them . . . You just have to bring her back."

Reaching up, I peeled her hand off my shirt and shoved her away from me. "I'll find her, and I'll bring her back. But you. Are. *Done*." I hissed, stabbing my finger in her face. "I warned you what would happen if you didn't take care of her the way you should. Now I'm gonna make sure you never fuckin' see her again."

"You—you can't do that! She's my daughter."

"Not anymore," I seethed. "You've never been good enough for her, and I'm done standing back while you ruin that girl. From this moment on, she's mine, and if you don't want me to ruin what little you have left of your pathetic life, you'll disappear."

"But—but we're family. Pope, I'm your sister."

"That's where you're wrong. You're nothing to me. Not anymore." Whipping around, I started away from her, ignoring her desperate pleas as she called my name. "Get her the fuck outta here," I said to Rake who was standing nearby. He nodded, and without saying a word, got to moving as I turned my focus on Bane, who was sitting at the bar that stretched across the entire back wall of the clubhouse, his fingers flying over his laptop. "Tell me what you got."

He lifted his head from the screen, the smile on his face enough to make a man's balls shrivel up inside his body. Bane's scary side had officially been engaged, and he was ready to get to work.

"Got property records for everything in Grant Wilfred's name. Includin' a secluded cabin about thirty minutes outside Redemption. Also managed to hack his phone, and it's pingin' at that same address."

"Good." I lifted my hand and circled my finger in the air. "You, Roe and Rake, with me. Let roll out."

I'd forgotten I still had Lennon's hand in mine until she gave it a slight jerk, bringing my focus back around to her. Popping up on her toes, she pressed a kiss to my lips and whispered, "Be safe. I'll be here when you get back."

TWENTY-SEVEN
POPE

A DILAPIDATED SHACK would have been a more apt description for Grant Wilfred's cabin in the middle of nowhere. The place looked like it was one strong gust of wind away from crumbling to the ground.

It had taken way too long for us to get here. Like Angela said, the cabin was about an hour away, and while my men and I managed to shave precious minutes off that time, we'd lost it again when we had to ditch our bikes a mile back on the narrow road that led up here and make the rest of it on foot to keep from alerting Wilfred to our presence.

Now that we were outside the cabin, it took everything in me to keep from planting my boot in the door and kicking it open. We needed a plan. While Bane and Rake kept an eye on the front, Roe and I quietly circled the structure, peeking in windows, trying to get the lay of things while looking for Marigold.

I didn't know what I was going to do if she wasn't there. The thought that I might never find her flashed through my brain, but before it had a chance to cripple me, Roe was there, clapping me on the shoulder and pulling me from those miserable thoughts. "She's here, brother," he assured me. "She's here, and we're gonna get her out."

I nodded, shaking off the black clouds trying to suffocate me. I kept low as we crept silently around the house. The side window looked into the kitchen with a straight shot into what was most likely the living room. From that vantage point, I could make out Wilfred pacing the length of the small room as he waved an arm in the air, ranting to someone on the phone he held to his ear. I memorized the layout then continued on. When we got to a window at the back of the house, I popped up, seeing a bedroom with nothing more than a small cot, and in the center of it, I caught a flash of familiar blonde hair I'd know anywhere. I held my breath as I watched, silently sending a prayer to whoever was listening to give me a sign of life, *something* to show me she was okay.

As though someone was listening, Marigold rolled onto her back on the cot. From what I could see, her wrists and ankles were bound, but she was alive. She was here, and she was alive.

For the first time in hours, I was able to take a full deep breath. Since the moment Pops collapsed, it felt like someone had been clenching my lungs in their fists. But that flash of golden sunshine was all I needed.

I lowered back into a crouch and signaled for Roe to follow me, and together, we snuck back to the front of the house to meet up with Rake and Bane.

"She's in there," I announced, taking in the sighs of relief from my brothers as soon as the words passed my lips. "Room at the very back."

Rake crossed his arms over his barrel chest. "So how do you want to play this?"

I looked to my second-in-command, the one man I trusted above all else. "Roe, I want you to get her out." He nodded and waited for me to continue. "She's tied up on a cot in the middle of the room. While you sneak around to the back, the three of us will wait here. Wilfred's in the living room, right inside the front door. What I want you to do is shatter the window. Make it loud so we can hear it up here. Once we do, we enter through the front. There won't be enough time for him to get from the front of the cabin to that room before we bust in. I don't want you to wait. As soon as you get Marigold, I want you to get her the fuck outta here, you understand? I want her as far away as you can carry her while we take care of Wilfred. She's been through enough. I don't want her witnessin' anything more."

He jerked his chin. "You got my word. I'll get her out and get her clear."

I didn't have a doubt in my mind that he would. It was why I'd trusted him with the task in the first place. He knew that girl in there was the most precious thing to me, but he also loved her almost as much as I did, and he'd step in front of a bullet if it meant keeping her safe.

I looked around at the three sets of eyes trained on me. My brothers, the men who'd had my back when I went through hell in an effort to pull our club out of it.

"Everyone ready?"

I got three nods and lifted my chin in return. As Roe bent low and moved silently to the back of the house, the rest of us headed toward the door. Bane and Rake had their backs pressed against the filthy wall on either side of the rickety frame, guns drawn, while I waited in front of it, my own Glock at the ready, poised to plant my boot in the middle of the rotting wood as soon as I heard the sound of breaking glass.

My heart pounded against my ribs so hard I thought the damn organ might bruise as I waited. It felt like it took forever, but in reality, it was probably only a minute before the sound of shattering glass echoed through the air like a gunshot. I moved immediately, lifting my leg and kicking the door open before the man inside had a chance to comprehend what the fuck was going on.

"What the fuck," he bellowed as Rake and Bane rushed in, guns lifted in his direction. I came in on their heels, squeezing the trigger and putting a bullet in the fucker's thigh before he had a chance to pull his own gun from the waistband of his pants.

He went down on a pained bellow, clutching at the wound. "What the *fuck*!" he repeated, his slow-ass brain still having trouble processing what had happened. I didn't have to look back to know Roe had done exactly as I'd instructed and was currently on the way back to where we'd parked with my niece in tow.

Feeling the relief from that, I moved toward the piece-of-shit on the ground.

"Ah, ah, ah," Rake warned when the fat bastard went for his gun at the sight of me. He planted the sole of his boot in the middle of Wilfred's face, breaking his nose and sending him sprawling to his back before landing another kick to the man's ribs, forcing him to roll onto his side and divesting him of his gun. "You won't be needin' this."

The two of them stood, guns trained on the man, ready to fire if they needed to, while I lowered to a crouch in front of him.

"You never should have fucked with my family," I told him, my lips curling back in a vicious smile at the sight of his cheeks turning ruddy. "Now you'll pay."

"Fuck you," he hissed, all bluster, even when he knew this was the end for him. But that didn't mean I couldn't see the fear in his eyes.

"Hope you can come up with something more creative than that as your last words."

I rose to my full height and took a step back, my gaze going to Bane. As badly as I wanted to stay here and make sure this piece of shit suffered an agony worse than death for what he'd done, I needed to get to Marigold. I needed to see with my own two eyes that she was safe, needed to hold her in my arms and feel her breathe. So I jerked my chin at the only man on the face of the earth who was capable of making me feel fear. "Make it hurt worse than you ever have before," I instructed. "And make it fuckin' last before you finish him."

He nodded in understanding, then looked down at the man on the floor with a smile that damn near froze my blood.

With that, I turned and marched out of the cabin, heading toward my girl. But as I moved in her direction, I couldn't help but smile when I heard the agonized screams coming from the cabin behind me.

Lennon

I lost track of time as I paced the length of the Iron Wraith's clubhouse over and over. My nerves were fried, but I couldn't sit still. I was worried about Marigold. I was worried about Pope and his men. I was worried about Pops.

The guys who'd been tasked with staying behind with me had been getting regular updates from a couple of the other members who were at the hospital, and apparently, Pops had come through his surgery without any complications and was doing fine, but I wasn't going to be able to relax until I could see him for myself.

Phoebe and Iris both had called to check in more than once, and while I appreciated my friends looking out for me and the people I cared about, I wasn't going to be able to calm down until this nightmare was over.

"You look like you could use a shot, Snow White," the brother behind the bar stated. He had a friendly grin and a mop of dirty-blond hair, a few shades darker than Pope's. He'd introduced himself to me as Gage, but I'd been too anxious to hold a conversation with him, not that he seemed to mind.

I gave him a shaky smile and shook my head. "Thanks, but I'm good."

"Sweetheart, you're anything but good. You're about to wear a hole right through the floor."

I let out a shaky breath and reached up to pull a trembling hand through my hair as I moved to one of the barstools across from where Gage was standing. "Sorry. I'm freaking out."

"Understandable." He pulled a beer from a cooler behind the bar, popped the cap, and slid it my way. "If you won't take a shot, at least drink that. It'll help take the edge off."

I wasn't so sure I believed him, but I took a drink anyway, offering him a grateful smile. "Thanks, I appreciate that."

"No problem."

"Have you heard anything yet?" I asked for what had to have been the millionth time. But if he was annoyed with me asking, he didn't let on. "Not yet. But I'm sure we'll have news soon."

I nodded, curling my lips between my teeth and biting down to keep from crying. Sensing I was only moments away from losing it, Gage reached across the bar and patted my hand, the black metal of his wedding band glinting beneath the light. "He'll get her. Don't worry. It'll all be okay."

I opened my mouth to agree, but before the words came out, the door to the clubhouse opened, and Pope came walking in.

I jumped off the barstool and bolted in his direction, but before I reached him, I spotted Marigold at his side and changed direction. Her dark eyes went wide at the sight of me, and as soon as I was close enough she lunged. On a sob, she crashed into me, wrapping her arms around my waist and burying her face in my neck.

"It's okay," I whispered, my own tears spilling down my cheeks as I clutched her tightly, holding her steady as her entire body wracked with sobs. "It's okay, sweet girl. You're safe. We have you," I assured her. "And we're never letting you go."

I planted a kiss on the side of her head, content to hold on to her as long as she needed, and lifted my gaze to the man in front of me. He was staring at me and Marigold, those fathomless eyes so full of love as he watched the two of us holding each other up.

"*I love you,*" I mouthed once his gaze connected with mine.

His nostrils flared and his chest expanded on a sharp inhale, and a second later, he mouthed back, "*I love you too, Raven.*"

Then he moved in, his big, strong arms wrapping around the both of us. Holding us close and keeping us safe. Just like I knew he always would.

Because that was just the type of man Courtland Pope was.

EPILOGUE

LENNON

ONE WEEK LATER

"I promise, sweetheart, I'm just fine."

I gave Pops a hard, unwavering look as I stared him down in his hospital bed. It had been a week since his surgery, and while he was on the mend, he still had quite a ways to go. He still didn't have his color back, and he looked like he'd lost too much weight.

"You had a *heart attack*," I stressed, using the same voice I used on my students when they were really pissing me off. "You could have died, and I walked in here and caught Rake giving you a bag from Burger Hut."

The man actually had the audacity to pout. "You can't

expect me to live off this hospital food," he whined. "A man could starve to death!"

"Hospital food never killed anyone," I rebutted, then shoved my finger at the bag Rake was still holding. "But the stuff in there sure as hell has." I cast Rake a death glare and ordered, "Get that stuff out of here."

He threw me a salute and started for the door to Pops's hospital room.

"Are you kiddin'?" Pops barked at his back. "You chickenshit!"

"Hell yeah," Rake said with a laugh. "She's a middle school teacher *by choice*. She's fuckin' terrifying."

I grinned proudly as I looked at Pops, planting my hands on my hips. I'd gotten to know Pope's brothers a lot better in the past several days, especially since almost all of them came by the house regularly to check on Marigold and make sure she was all right.

Some people might have thought they were scary because of the patch they wore, but I'd seen the real Iron Wraiths over the past week. I'd seen their heart. Their loyalty to the family they chose. And I knew the truth about them. They were good men. They might have done bad things, but to their core, they were good. Even Bane.

With the men checking and showing they cared, along with Pope and me to lean on, Marigold was doing a lot better than I had expected. It helped that one of the brothers was married to a licensed therapist. She'd offered her services, and I'd jumped at that. Marigold had seen her twice so far, and it seemed talking about what happened was helping.

The silver lining in the whole thing was that Grant Wilfred hadn't touched her. At least not in that way. But she'd witnessed him beating her mother and was kidnapped, scared out of her mind by the son of a bitch, so she still had scars from those two days.

I wasn't sure if it was normal or not, but she'd yet to ask about her mother. I intended to ask her therapist if that was something Pope and I needed to discuss but had decided to take it one day at a time. Eventually, we'd sit down and tell her the truth. Angela was gone and she'd be living with us from here on out. But we both agreed she didn't need to know her mother had taken off nearly the instant she was thrown out of the clubhouse. Pope's attorney was already working on getting Pope full custody on the grounds of abandonment.

One thing that had gone a long way in helping Marigold was the fact that Grant Wilfred's body had been found two days after Pope had rescued her and brought her home, so she knew he was never coming back for her.

Thanks to Bane, news of his corruption had hit the airwaves at the same time as his death, and the media reported that it looked like a hit from the criminal organization he'd been working for. Of course, Chief Brady held a press conference stating his shock and disappointment that one of his cops was corrupt and assured everyone it was only one bad apple, and the Ashland police department was committed to serving and protecting their community.

But everyone knew the truth; the rumblings all over town whispered that Wilfred was probably the tip of the iceberg.

I didn't doubt it, but for now, things in my little world were good. I had my man, we had our girl, and my circle of friends grew bigger by the day.

Pope's chuckle pulled me from my thoughts as his arm wrapped around my waist. "Come on, Raven. Let's leave the old man in peace. You can come torture him another day."

I leaned down and placed a kiss to Pops's cheek. "See you soon. Take care of yourself, okay?"

He smiled warmly. "You got it, Snow White." I rolled my eyes at his nickname for me and let Pope lead me out of the hospital room on Pops's chuckle.

The hallways were full of men in Wraith's patches, each one waiting for their turn to see Pops, as was the case every day since his heart attack.

Pope slapped hands and bumped knuckles with a few of them as we walked by on the way to the elevator.

Before we could reach it, it dinged and the doors slid open. I felt Pope go stiff at my side and heard him let out mumbled curse when a beautiful blonde woman stepped out and turned in our direction. The instant her gaze landed on Pope—or more importantly, the vest he was wearing—the worry that had marred her pretty face gave way to anger.

She stomped in our direction, exuding a pissed-off air, catching the attention of the men around us.

"Who's that?" I whispered under my breath.

"That's Dakota Riley," he returned just as quietly. "Pops's daughter."

Oh shit.

She stopped two feet away and planted her hands on her hips. "Pope," she greeted, that one word cold enough to turn a person to ice.

"Dakota," he returned, his greeting much warmer. "It's good to have you back."

"Can't say I agree," she clipped. "And I'm not back. I'm only here until my dad gets back on his feet, then I'm gone."

"Well, I know he'll be real happy to see you."

She didn't say anything to that, leading me to believe there was some bad blood somewhere down the line. Instead, she said, "Let's get one thing straight. While I'm here, I don't want to have a damn thing to do with your club, got it? I've got nothing to say to any of you, so you'd do best to stay the hell out of my way."

With that, she shoved past him and stomped down the hall in the direction of her father's room, ignoring every one of the men watching her.

"What was *that* about?" I asked once I managed to pick my jaw up off the floor.

Pope let out a sigh and reached around to rub at the back of his neck. "Long story. Just know, you shouldn't judge her based on that impression, Raven. Dakota's a good person. There's just a lot of history there."

I let him guide me to the elevators, however I couldn't help looking back over my shoulder. My gaze moved from the woman's retreating form to Roe, who was standing stock-still in the middle of the hallway like he'd seen a ghost. And as I watched, the expression on his face shifted from shock to one of longing.

Interesting. Very, *very* interesting.

Pope

> *Two months later*

.   .   .

I was met with the sound of laughter as soon as I pushed the door open and stepped into the house. "I'm here," I called out. "Where's everyone at?"

"In the kitchen," Lennon returned, her voice full of laughter.

I headed in that direction, running into Otto first as he closed the door to the fridge and passed me the beer he'd just pulled out.

I popped the top and lifted it in salute. "Appreciate it. It's been a long day."

Work at the garage hadn't slowed down. If anything, it was getting busier. There were more custom jobs lined up than ever, and it looked like I was going to have to bring more people in to handle the day-to-day so my guys could focus on the builds.

"Well, you're in for a treat. Esther and Marigold have been cookin' up a feast. We'll be eating good tonight."

Since the night I packed Lennon up and took her home with me, she hadn't been back to her house. We'd discussed what to do with the little bungalow, and eventually decided that, instead of selling it, she'd rent it out. That way she could control who moved onto the street. She might not live there anymore, but she was still very protective of her crew, and she didn't want to stick them with a shitty neighbor. More people had applied than she'd expected, but she'd managed to find something wrong with every single one of them.

Until last week's applicant.

She was still close with all of them, especially Otto and Esther, who had become more like family, so once a week, we headed to their house for dinner. It turned out, the couple was just what my Goldie needed as well, because under their tender care, she'd started to blossom. The nightmares were nearly gone, and my happy, sunny girl was back. If Lennon and I were like her parents, Esther and Otto were the grandparents of her heart, and the two of them seemed more than happy to wear that title with pride.

I moved to my woman, wrapping my hand at her throat and using my thumb to tip her face up for a kiss. She beamed at me. "Hi, honey," she said gently.

"Hey, baby. You have a good day?"

"Every day's a good day," she answered, making me feel ten feet tall and bulletproof.

"Don't I know it," I returned before moving over to my girl and wrapping and arm around her shoulders. I pressed a kiss to the crown of her head and inhaled her sunshine.

"Hey, Unka," she greeted with a giggle.

"Hey, sweetheart."

She reached for the stack of plates sitting on the counter and shoved them into my stomach. "Dinner's almost ready, so you set the table."

I chuckled, placing my beer on the counter and

giving her a salute as I grabbed the plates and cutlery. "Yes, ma'am."

Once we were all sitting down to eat, I turned to Otto and gave him a knowing smile before asking, "So how's the new neighbor workin' out?"

The old man chuckled, giving his head a shake. "She's a good girl, fits in well with everyone, but she'll make things interesting, that's for sure."

Oh I just bet she would.

On that thought, the doorbell rang, and Marigold's entire face lit up. She bounced in her chair before looking at me. "Can I answer it, Unka? *Please*?"

My chest shook on a silent laugh. "Go ahead."

She bolted out of the dining room, and a second later I heard her squeal of delight, followed by, "Hark! You came to visit me!"

I lifted my gaze, a smile stretching my lips wide, and when I looked at Lennon across the table from me, she was already looking at me, a matching smile on her beautiful face.

"*I love you*," she mouthed before lifting her wineglass and taking a sip.

"*I love you too, Raven*," I returned.

Then, without her noticing, I reached beneath the table and patted my front pocket, making sure the ring I'd tucked in there earlier was still safe and sound.

She didn't know it yet, but later tonight, I had every

intension of making that woman mine for the rest of our lives.

And I couldn't wait.

The End.

I really hope you enjoyed Pope's story, and I can't wait to give you more from Ashland!

SNEAK PEAK OF BAD ALIBI

Want to know where Pope was first introduced? Check out book 1 in my Redemption series, *BAD ALIBI*, now!

Chapter 1
Farah

Stepping across the threshold into the entryway of the old Victorian, I was hit with the smells of wood rot and mold.

I was far from an expert when it came to construction, but considering the state the house was in, I wouldn't have been surprised to learn the whole place needed to be ripped down to the studs.

And that didn't bother me one damn bit.

"Uh, Ms. Hyland?"

At my realtor's voice, I stopped gazing around and turned my attention to him. "Please, call me Farah."

"Okay, Farah. I have to admit, I was more than a little surprised when you asked to view this property." He looked around at the rambling pile of rubble with undisguised dismay. "It's . . . well, a disaster, really."

"It's not a disaster, Mr. Clark," I insisted, taking in what was probably a stunning parlor back in the day. Where the tin ceiling tiles probably once added character, they were now completely covered in rust. The gaudy floral wallpaper was peeling, and rodents had eaten holes in the drywall, exposing wiring that would undoubtedly fail inspection. What was once a gorgeous home had been abandoned, left to rot away. "It's a fixer-upper."

"That may be. But with your budget, you can easily afford a place that's move-in ready. This . . . this will take a *lot* of work."

I knew he was trying to talk me out of the place, but I felt a sense of belonging in this house. It had been neglected far too long, just like me. With the help of the two people I held most dearly, I'd been able to pull myself up and put the pieces of my tattered life back together, and now that I was strong enough, I was going to offer this old girl the same chance.

The shape of the house might have been a deterrent to most people, but to me, the challenge made my blood sing and filled me with excitement.

I was a twenty-six-year-old woman who, until recently, had never had to work for anything. All my life, I'd had things handed to me on a silver platter. But those things came with a million strings attached, and the saddest part was, most of what I had, I'd never wanted in the first place.

Just like every generation before me for as long as I could trace back, I'd been born and raised in Connecticut, living the entitled life that came with the Hyland name. My great-great-grandfather had struck it big in steel, setting my family up to be one of the richest in all of New England. The Hyland's were the very definition of old money, and with the name came expectations I'd always hated.

From the time I came into this world, my entire life had been planned for me. Everything from what college I'd attend and what I'd major in to the man I'd eventually marry had all been chosen without my say. Hylands didn't make waves. We were expected to sit back, keep our mouths shut, and just go with it. But because I had a mind of my own and dared to question my parents' plans for me, I was labeled the black sheep of the family.

All my relatives looked down their noses at me, snickering and whispering behind my back at family events.

As far as my parents were concerned, I was a stain on the family name. I was the daughter of Geoffrey and Margo Hyland, for God's sake. My father was the oldest son and heir to the Hyland Steel fortune. I was to do as they said without batting an eye, and the fact that I believed I should have a say in my future made me a huge disappointment to them—something they'd begun making all too clear to me as soon as I was old enough to understand words.

After so many years of having my own parents despise me, that strong will I'd been born with had been beaten into submission. I stopped thinking about what *I* wanted and became the obedient daughter they'd always desired.

I attended Cornell University because that was where *they* wanted me to go and got a worthless degree in Fine

Arts because *they* deemed it appropriate. After all, it wouldn't do for a Hyland woman not to be educated, but we weren't actually supposed to work. It was our job to marry money, pop out babies, and volunteer on the boards of several *respectable* charities.

I'd begun dating Lance Maryweather, the son of my parents' best friends, not because I was attracted to him, but because it had been arranged by our families. And when he proposed the winter before last, I'd said yes because, according to my father, it was a wise business move, having the princess of a steel fortune married to the heir of a line of thriving department stores.

We'd been set for a spring wedding, because spring was the ideal time for a lavish outdoor wedding for the upper crust of society. Our mothers had been in fits, planning the wedding of the century, and for months it was all anyone could talk about. Everyone who was anyone would be in attendance, and I was going to be the envy of all the women in my social circle. Or at least that had been the plan.

Then one night had changed everything in a way that was irreversible. It had changed *me*. But then, nearly dying had a tendency to do that to a person.

I woke up in that hospital bed a broken shell of my former self. It had taken months to pull myself together, but once I had, I knew I'd been given a second chance, and there was no way I was letting it go to waste.

Starting fresh hadn't been easy. Cutting ties that had kept me tethered to a life I never liked nor wanted had been an arduous task, but I'd done it. Breaking things off with Lance had been the easiest part. Truth was, knowing I wouldn't be stuck with him for the rest of my life was a serious weight lifted off my chest, but my parents were a different story. In spite of how they'd made me feel growing up, I still craved their approval. They were my blood, and having them turn their backs on me hurt more than I could have imagined.

I guess, in the back of my mind, I'd held out hope that they would understand why I needed to do what I'd done. But I'd been wrong.

By the time I'd finished shaking off the dregs of my old life, I only had two people left to support me. Fortunately, they were more than enough. With their help, I held on to the strength I needed to start this next chapter of my life.

I was a whole new Farah. Granted, I was a new Farah who didn't have the first clue what she wanted to do with her new life, but still, it was exhilarating to have the chance, and I wasn't going to squander it.

Turning back to my realtor, I felt my lips tug up in a smile so big it made my cheeks ache. "Anything worth having is worth putting in the work, Mr. Clark. Make an offer."

He raised one brow, giving me an incredulous look. "You're sure?"

"Oh yeah." Tipping my head back, I scanned the house that would hopefully soon become my home, feeling an unfamiliar warmth begin to unfurl in my chest. "I'm absolutely positive."

ACKNOWLEDGMENTS

To Josh and Jacob. I love you both like crazy.

To my family, thank you so much for the unwavering support.

To Adriana, Dylan, Bella, Jill, and Jennifer. I'm not sure I'll every be able to write without you ever again. PLEASE DON'T LEAVE ME!

To Tia, Laura, Amy, Amy, and Kandi. Thank you so much for your friendship.

To Karen and Jan, for taking my words and making them into something understandable, and for not firing me when I blow through EVERY SINGLE deadline.

To my ARC team and all my readers, I wouldn't be here if it wasn't for you. Thank you so much for loving my words as much as I do and sticking with me all this time. Here's to more to come!

JESSICA'S PRINCESSES

Come be a part of Jessica's Princesses Reader Group, where you'll get first looks at cover reveals, what's coming next, and so much more.

Jessica's Princesses

ABOUT JESSICA

Born and raised around Houston. Jessica is a self proclaimed caffeine addict, connoisseur of inexpensive wine, and the worst driver in the state of Texas. In addition to being all of these things, she's first and foremost a wife and mom.

Growing up, she shared her mom and grandmother's love of reading. But where they leaned toward murder mysteries, Jessica was obsessed with all things romance.

When she's not nose deep in her next manuscript, you can usually find her with her kindle in hand.

Connect with Jessica now
Website: www.authorjessicaprince.com
Jessica's Princesses Reader Group
Newsletter
Instagram
Facebook
Twitter
authorjessicaprince@gmail.com